Cha X
Charyn, Jerome.
Citizen Sidel

$ 23.00

CITIZEN SIDEL

BOOKS BY JEROME CHARYN

CITIZEN SIDEL
DEATH OF A TANGO KING
THE DARK LADY FROM BELORUSSE
EL BRONX
LITTLE ANGEL STREET
MONTEZUMA'S MAN
BACK TO BATAAN
MARIA'S GIRLS
ELSINORE
THE GOOD POLICEMAN
MOVIELAND
PARADISE MAN
METROPOLIS
WAR CRIES OVER AVENUE C
PINOCCHIO'S NOSE
PANNA MARIA
DARLIN' BILL
THE CATFISH MAN
THE SEVENTH BABE
SECRET ISAAC
THE FRANKLIN SCARE
THE EDUCATION OF PATRICK SILVER
MARILYN THE WILD
BLUE EYES
THE TAR BABY
EISENHOWER, MY EISENHOWER
AMERICAN SCRAPBOOK
GOING TO JERUSALEM
THE MAN WHO GREW YOUNGER
ON THE DARKENING GREEN
ONCE UPON A DROSHKY

EDITED BY JEROME CHARYN

THE NEW MYSTERY

JEROME CHARYN

CITIZEN SIDEL

THE MYSTERIOUS PRESS

Published by Warner Books

A Time Warner Company

Mysterious Press books are published by Warner Books, Inc., 1271 Avenue of the
America, New York, NY 10020.

Visit our Web site at http://warnerbooks.com

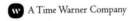 A Time Warner Company

The Mysterious Press name and logo are registered trademarks of Warner Books, Inc.

Printed in the United States of America

First printing: January 1999

10 9 8 7 6 5 4 3 2 1

Library of Congress Cataloging-in-Publication Data

Charyn, Jerome.
    Citizen Sidel / Jerome Charyn.
        p.   cm.
    ISBN 0-89296-605-X
    I. Title.
PS3553.H33C43 1998
813'.54—dc21   98-16360
                                                                 CIP

Part One

I

He was the Democrats' darling, Isaac Sidel, mayor of New York and ex–police commissioner, about to be picked as the Party's vice-presidential candidate. He was going to run with J. Michael Storm, the baseball czar, who'd defeated senators and billionaires in the primaries. J. Michael had settled the worst strike in the history of baseball. He was a ferocious candidate . . . and a former student radical, whom Isaac himself had kept out of jail. The country had fallen in love with them. They were their own kind of comedy team: Laurel and Hardy had come back to life as a pair of mischievous commandoes. But Isaac didn't have time for comedy. The town was swollen with Democrats, and Isaac was the babysitter and sheriff of the Democratic Convention.

The Party had captured Madison Square Garden in the middle of a heat wave; Isaac had to worry about mad bombers, demonstrators, and air-conditioning ducts. He also had to sit with the New York delegation, act like a pol, shake the hands of Democrats who wanted to *feel* the future vice-president. He'd been on the cover of *Time* magazine with J. Michael. He'd sat with journalists from India, Hong Kong, Spain . . . he had ten or twenty interviews each hour. Reporters couldn't stop pestering him.

Isaac had his own Secret Service man, who would officially belong to him once J. Michael received the nomination and declared his running mate to the whole convention. Isaac couldn't get rid of his federal shadow, Martin Boyle, a thirty-two-year-old marksman from Oklahoma City who liked to talk guns and horses and girls with Sidel. Boyle was six foot two and had been trained to step in front of a bullet, give his own life for whatever candidate he had to protect.

"Mr. President . . ."

"Damn you, Boyle," Isaac said. "Are you dreaming me into the White House? A vice-president is always the Party's forgotten man, and what if J. and me lose the election?"

"Sir," said Martin Boyle, "look all around you . . . you're the real meat on the Democratic ticket."

"Don't say that, Boyle. You'll jinx J. Michael."

"He's already jinxed . . . haven't you read his file, sir? He's so fucking compromised, he won't last six months on Pennsylvania Avenue."

"Then why haven't the Republicans torn his teeth out?"

"They'd rather battle J. Michael than 'The Citizen' . . . that's your code name with the Service. It's a sign of deep respect."

"And what do you call J. Michael?"

"Shitman."

"Will you call him that once he's elected?"

"Among ourselves? Yes."

"Would you like a change of scenery, Boyle? Would you like to watch the whole fucking Secret Service get flopped?"

"No, sir."

"Then close your mouth, and quit dogging me. Michael could still change his mind and pick another vice-president. I'm only Citizen Sidel."

He ran away from Boyle and left Madison Square Garden. The metal detectors went berserk. Isaac was wearing his Glock. That was one of his attractions to the American people: a possible vice-president who packed a gun inside his pants, like a highwayman or a police chief, and Isaac had been both.

He wasn't thinking about security at the Garden, or the delegates that J. Michael still had to win . . . it was a captain who'd worked with Isaac at One Police Plaza, an exemplary cop close to retirement; Douglas Knight was accused of killing his own son, also a cop, decorated like his dad with medals for bravery. There'd been some talk before the shooting, that Internal Affairs was investigating father and son, that Doug and Doug Jr. had gone into business for themselves, were moonlighting as hitmen. Isaac couldn't believe it. He'd watched Doug Jr. grow up, saw his devotion to the NYPD.

The captain was in a cell at the Criminal Courts Building. Wouldn't even talk to his wife. He was sitting there in the dark, like a man without a country. Isaac should have been pumping hands at the convention, conferring with Tim Seligman, Party strategist, the kingmaker who would stand behind J. Michael's throne, whisper in his ear. Tim had been paging Isaac, had wanted him to mingle with hardnosed delegates from the South, who weren't so happy with the thought of "a

Hebrew vice-president." But Isaac couldn't mingle right now. And he could barely get away from the Garden. Democratic wives, out on a shopping spree, trapped Isaac as he was crossing Seventh Avenue.

"Mr. President," they said, and Isaac began to wonder if Tim Seligman was hatching some dirty plot to get rid of J. at the last moment and thrust Citizen Sidel upon the convention.

"Important business," he told the wives and hopped into a cab. The driver demanded Isaac's autograph. "Your Honor, you'd make a better president than that bum. Let him stick to baseball."

Isaac rushed out of the cab, beeped his chauffeur, and arrived at Criminal Courts in the mayor's official wagon. He went into the basement, asked for Captain Knight. The jailor insisted Knight wouldn't see him.

"That's fine," Isaac said, and walked with the jailor into the little compound of cells. The captain groaned when he saw Isaac.

"Are you the devil, Mr. Mayor?"

"Not all the time."

"Then will you leave me to rot in peace?"

"Can't do that, Doug. You'll have to talk to me."

The captain's bitter smile broke through the black bars of his cell.

"I can wait you out, Isaac. You're in the thick of a convention, with all the hurlyburly. You're the Democrats' man."

"Fuck the convention, and fuck the hurlyburly. I'll be with you, Doug. Night and day. I like long vigils."

The captain nodded to his jailor, who unlocked the cell,

and they all marched out of the cellblock. Isaac rode upstairs with Captain Knight to a judge who let him borrow his chambers; they sat among a mountain of law books.

"I killed him," the captain said. "Isn't that enough?"

"You're a cop," Isaac whispered, "one of the best I ever had, and cops don't kill their sons . . . there had to be a reason."

"Haven't you heard the rumors? Jr. and I had our own little assassination bureau. We were doing hits for the Maf. We had a falling-out. Over the millions we made, of course. He wanted to whack me, and I whacked him first."

The captain started to cry.

"Now what the fuck happened?" Isaac said.

"He was taking money . . . doing favors he shouldn't have done. He was up to his ass in debt."

"Loan sharks?" Isaac asked.

"Loan sharks. Other cops. Girlfriends, grocers, anybody he could grab from."

"And what sort of favors did he do?"

"He'd ride shotgun for a couple of bad guys."

"Okay, but that's not a capital crime. You didn't kill Jr. for babysitting Mafia money. It's the number-one job for retired cops . . . babysitting."

"But Jr. wasn't retired. He was thirty-three. I finished him. It would only have gotten worse. Mr. Mayor, can I go back to my cell, please . . ."

Seligman kept paging him. The Democrats needed Sidel. But the captain's story didn't make sense. Isaac rode across the Brooklyn Bridge and paid a visit to the captain's wife on Pineapple Street. He solved half the mystery before Sandra

Knight uttered a word. She had bruises under both her eyes. Her mouth was swollen. She still kept the chain-guard on, and Isaac had to peek at her through the crack in the door that the chain allowed.

"Sandra," he said. "I'm not a robber. Let me in."

She slid the chain off its clasp, and Isaac squeezed past Sandra Knight.

"Isaac, forgive me," she said. "There were reporters . . . and cops in plain clothes."

"Internal," Isaac said. "They're nosing around. That's their job."

"My boy isn't even buried yet . . . and my husband is already far away. He blames me," Sandra said.

"You were lending Jr. money behind Doug's back, weren't you? Lots of money."

"I had to . . . he said they would kill him."

"*They?*"

"Gangsters. Other cops. I'm not sure. He got crazier and crazier."

"Then it wasn't the first time Jr. hit you."

"I had no more money to give him."

"And Doug warned him, that if he ever . . ."

"It wasn't a warning," Sandra said. "Nothing like that. But Doug came home, saw the marks on my face, found Jr. . . . and shot him dead."

Isaac stood outside Poplar Street, the home of Internal Affairs. He didn't dare meddle. He was only the mayor. He waited, shuffled his feet, until a detective he knew waltzed out of the building. Isaac couldn't have used the telephone. All the lines at Internal were tapped. He followed the detective a couple of blocks, caught up with him, grabbed his arm. "Hello, Herman."

The detective blinked. "Your Honor?"

"Walk a little way with me, Herm."

Herman Broadman had once played center field on the Delancey Giants, Isaac's team at the Police Athletic League. And Broadman had graduated from PAL to the NYPD and a detective's slot at Internal Affairs.

"I need a big fucking favor," Isaac said.

"Boss, don't compromise me . . . I'd have to handcuff you in the middle of the street."

"I don't want to tilt the evidence, nothing like that. But I need to know about Doug Jr."

"I won't unlock information."

"Herm, please. Just a hint. Did he have a particular sweetheart?"

"Come on, Isaac, tell me what you'll do for me once you're President of the United States . . . a cabinet post, huh?"

"I'm not practicing for the presidency, Herm. And I have nothing to give. I just hope Captain Knight doesn't die like a dog."

"Was I your best center fielder, Isaac?"

"No, Herm. You didn't have the moves, and you didn't have the stick. But you were a hell of a hustler."

"I love you, Isaac. You never bullshitted me . . . wait here."

Isaac licked his thumbs for half an hour, had to hide his nervousness. His chauffeur found him with a finger in his mouth. "Mr. Mayor, Tim Seligman's been calling on the car phone . . . there's a crisis. Something about Southern delegates you'll have to woo."

"Mullins," he said to his chauffeur, a retired cop with heart problems and a hernia (Isaac loved to hire invalids). "You tell Tim that Isaac Sidel is invisible, that you can't get him on the horn."

"He'll cripple me, Isaac. He's boss of all the Democrats."

"In two days I'll be on the ticket. I'll eat Tim Seligman alive. Just play dumb."

"But I can't lie," Mullins said. "I met you, face to face . . ."

"Mullins, you can't meet an invisible man . . . good-bye."

The chauffeur disappeared, and Isaac continued to lick his thumbs until Broadman arrived.

"Well, Herm, who's the Mata Hari?"

"It's not that simple, boss."

"Ah, then tell me there's no bimbo involved . . . that Doug Jr. was only searching for pocket money."

"I didn't say there wasn't a woman, but she's not a bimbo."

"Are you an Indian giver, Herm? You promised me . . . what's her name?"

"Daniella."

"Daniella? Daniella what?"

"Daniella Grossvogel, a college professor . . . teaches comparative lit at NYU."

"Stop romancing me, Herm. Is she related to—"

"Yes. She's Captain Grossvogel's daughter."

"Grand," Isaac said. "Doug Jr. happens to be in love with his own captain's daughter. Or did Barton Grossvogel get bumped upstairs?"

"He's still captain of the oh-four."

"The prince of Elizabeth Street," Isaac said.

"He runs the tightest ship in Manhattan. All his detectives deliver."

"And IAD isn't investigating him, I suppose?"

"Isaac, that's none of your business . . . Daniella's teaching in the summer session. You can find her at NYU."

He was ashamed of himself. He used his popularity, his appeal as mayor and potential candidate, to barge into Daniella Grossvogel's class. He got her schedule from the registrar's office. Mata Hari, he muttered to himself, and took a seat. She was in her thirties, a short woman with a slight hump on her back . . . and a lovely face. Daniella's students recognized Sidel and the Glock he carried. Daniella had to pause in her lecture, quiet the classroom. She was talking about *another* Isaac, a scribbler named Isaac Babel, and the Maldavanka district in Odessa, where Babel's hero, Benya Krik, was born. Isaac began to cry. His own sweetheart, Margaret Tolstoy, aka Anastasia, had spent part of her childhood in Odessa. She'd lived like a cannibal during World War II, had swallowed the flesh of young boys from the local insane asylum to keep from starving.

"The Maldavanka was where anything could happen," said Daniella Grossvogel. "Babel used it as his own magic lantern . . . to invent Benya Krik, a most improbable gangster in orange pants."

She lost her concentration, stared at Isaac, and dismissed the class. Isaac slouched toward her like a penitent. She was no Mata Hari. Herm had been right.

"You're just like my father," she said. "A policeman who thinks he can go anywhere, enter any room."

"Professor Grossvogel, I didn't . . ."

"We were going to get married. A hunchback like me, a certified old maid. But we were lovers. Are you laughing, Mr. Mayor?"

"No, no. I understand your grief. I didn't mean to interrupt. But . . ."

"I couldn't even have a proper mourning period. The summer session is so short."

"But how did it happen? How did it reach a point where Captain Knight had to kill his own son?"

"Didn't you talk to my dad?"

"I couldn't. I didn't even learn about you until a little while ago. But why did young Doug need cash? He stole from his mom, beat her up. What was going down on Elizabeth Street?"

"Ask my father."

"Please," Isaac said. "I'm asking you."

"Greed," said Daniella. "My father runs the stationhouse like his own little corporation. I begged Doug to transfer, to get out, but he went deeper and deeper into the business of Elizabeth Street."

"Did he fight with his old man about it?"

"I'm not sure, but his father did talk to my father . . . a meeting of captains. There was a lot of shouting."

"Young Doug told you that?"

"He didn't have to tell. I was there . . . doing volunteer work. I would help a lot of policemen with their writing skills, prepare them for the sergeant's test. That's how I met

Doug. I was always a groupie at my father's different precincts. The captain's ugly duckling. I coached Doug. We fell in love . . ."

"Thanks, Professor Grossvogel."

"I'm not a professor. I haven't finished my Ph.D. I'm working on Isaac Babel, comparing him to Hemingway. They were both incredible stylists, don't you think? 'A period in the right place is like a hammer in the heart.' That's what Babel said . . ."

She was sobbing, and Isaac held her in his arms, rocked her gently, kissed her on the forehead.

He called Tim Seligman from a pay phone in the corridor. "Hello, Tim. Hold the fort. I have one more errand to do."

"Isaac, come home. The Southern boys are rebelling. We can't wrap up the convention. They'll stick to their favorite sons on the first ballot. And J. Michael will look like a fool."

"Then why don't you guarantee them that J. will choose another vice-president, that they don't have to live with a Hebe on the ticket?"

"We're not caving in," Tim said. "The convention will call J. a chickenshit. If he appears weak now, what will happen in November? I need you to charm Texas and Georgia and Mississippi."

"One more errand, Tim."

Isaac hung up the phone and hopped down to Elizabeth Street. There was a hush when he entered the main hall. He could have been Mr. Death, a walking skeleton with a Glock in his pants. No one acknowledged him, not the young cops or the band of prostitutes they'd brought in. Finally the desk sergeant told him, "Mr. Mayor, you'll have to park that pistol."

"I have a carry permit," Isaac said, like a sour little boy.

"But you're not a peace officer, and you can't wear a gun in this house."

Isaac deposited his Glock with the desk sergeant. "I'd like to see the captain. It's a courtesy call. Ring him for me, will ya?"

The sergeant telephoned upstairs. "Captain, the mayor's here . . . yes, sir. I will." He smiled with the phone in his hand. "You'll have to wait. The captain's very busy."

Isaac could have twisted the sergeant's nose and rushed upstairs, but he wasn't going to fight an entire precinct. Detectives stared at him, stood among themselves. And then Captain Grossvogel appeared at the top of the stairwell, with a Glock strapped to his chest, and waved to Isaac. He was a huge man, a former college wrestler and weight lifting champion of the NYPD. Isaac couldn't imagine him with a humpbacked daughter.

"Good to see you, Mr. Mayor. Come on up."

Isaac started to climb, but Grossvogel's detectives were in his way. The mayor had to march around them.

There'll be a reckoning, lads, he muttered to himself. *A lot of asses will get kicked on Elizabeth Street.*

He followed Grossvogel into his office, saw the captain's trophies.

"I was at NYU, Bart."

"Is that a fact?" Grossvogel said.

"I attended one of your daughter's lectures . . . she has the gift, a real gift."

"For literature, you mean. She's a bookish girl."

"Why did you rob her of a husband?"

The captain's neck muscles started to twitch. "Isaac," he said, "watch yourself. You're stepping into unfamiliar territories."

"Like your stationhouse, Bart?"

The twitching stopped, and Isaac understood the contempt those detectives on the stairs had for him. Elizabeth Street was the far country, beyond Isaac's reach. Grossvogel was a protected man. Attached to some fucking presidential commission? Or was he dancing with the FBI?

"You're a heavenly angel, aren't you, Bart? What was your fight with Doug Sr. about? . . . come on, Daniella told me that he visited the precinct."

"We had a chat. Just like me and you."

"Was he on to your shenanigans, Bart? Did he threaten to close you down? . . . and you sent young Doug after him, to cool off his own dad. Did Jr. owe you money? Did you set him up in some gambling sting?"

"Your Honor, you're hallucinating. You're out of control."

"Did you agree to sell your daughter to him for a certain price?"

Grossvogel reached across his desk to clutch Isaac's summer suit. The Citizen was wearing light colors in a heat wave, colors from Milan. He had to stop dressing like a bum.

"Your Honor, are you calling me a pimp?"

"Worse," Isaac said, with Grossvogel's thick fingers near his throat.

"Get away from me, or I'll rip you off at the neck and carry your fucking head in my pocket."

"You got the kid crazy, sent him to murder his old man . . ."

"Dream all you want. Play Sherlock Holmes. I don't give a shit."

"You will, Bart. You will. Whoever your rabbi is, I'll find him."

"Sure, Vice-President Sidel."

He was careless on his walk uptown. He landed on a deserted part of Crosby Street. A blue sedan appeared like a fat, lazy shark. He heard the shark's motor at the back of his mind. But he couldn't stop dreaming of Doug and Doug Jr. He was trying to choreograph a killing.

The blue sedan barreled down upon Isaac, and a body tackled him, knocked Isaac on his ass . . . and out of the car's fucking path. Isaac groaned. It was his Secret Service man, Martin Boyle.

"Boyle," Isaac said, "have you been following me? You weren't supposed to do that."

"I have my orders, Mr. President."

Three men wearing pillowcase masks, like the Ku Klux Klan, popped out of the car, clutching shotguns. Isaac groaned again. He was fond of Boyle. He didn't want his own Secret Service man to die of birdshot wounds, protecting Citizen Sidel. Isaac got off his ass, stood in front of Boyle.

"Sir," Boyle said, "you can't do that."

"But I am doing it."

Isaac took out his Glock and shot the trunk of the sedan. There was a terrific boom on that dead street. The men in pillowcase masks seemed uncertain now. People began to arrive from different corners, drawn to the sound of Isaac's Glock.

"Children," Isaac said to the three masked men, "you can go back to Elizabeth Street and tell your master that you saw 'The Citizen,' and 'The Citizen' doesn't scare."

The three men returned to their sedan, mumbled something, and drove away in their masks.

His Italian suit was dirty. His tie had been torn when Boyle tackled him. But Isaac wouldn't change his clothes. He arrived at the Garden with a hundred cameras in his face, Boyle half a step in front of him, already attached to Citizen Sidel. Reporters screamed at Isaac.

"Mr. Mayor, Mr. Mayor, was it an assassination attempt?"

There were already images of Isaac on the huge television screens inside the Garden. Commentators were interviewing witnesses of the shoot-out on Crosby Street.

"I couldn't believe it," a woman said. "Three men had come to kill our mayor. They wore masks. They wanted to butcher Isaac. But he's no schlemiel. He pulled out his gun . . ."

Tim Seligman grabbed him by the arm, kidnapped Isaac, led him into his own mandarin headquarters, under the air-conditioning ducts.

"Look at you," said the prince of the Party, who'd been a fighter pilot in Vietnam. "We're in a shitstorm, and Michael's running mate comes back to us in rags. We could lose the nomination in a single fucking nanosecond. That's how fast the weather changes."

"What can I do, Tim?"

"Dance. Entertain. Talk to delegates. Show them you're a regular guy."

"A regular guy?" Isaac said. "Manhattan doesn't breed regular guys."

"Then pretend a little, Your Honor."

"Timmy," Isaac said, "I can't. One of my policemen is sitting in a dark cell. He killed his own son. Another policeman drove him to it. Barton Grossvogel, captain of the fourth precinct. It's a fucking crime school, Tim. But some super-agency is protecting this Grossvogel."

"We'll close his crime school. But not today. Put on a fresh suit."

"No," Isaac said.

"We're hanging by a hair. If Mississippi and Texas shun J. on the first ballot, we'll lose momentum."

"Then why doesn't J. show up and shake a couple of hands?"

"It's a bad strategy. It will look like he's grubbing for votes. He can't appear until he clinches the nomination."

"But I can grub," Isaac said. "I can be the beggar."

"It's only natural. You're his running mate."

And they stepped out onto the fury of the convention floor. There were huge balloons of the Democratic donkey, the Party's favorite animal, floating above Isaac's head. He wasn't made for politics. He couldn't dance, he couldn't convince delegates.

Half the Mississippi delegation strode across the floor to welcome *their* vice-president. They'd watched Sidel on the huge television screens, wanted to discuss the shoot-out on Crosby Street. A whole little story began to boomerang off the Garden's walls. Isaac Sidel, Manhattan's favorite son, had left the convention floor to visit a policeman in distress. A mobbed-up captain, Isaac's mysterious enemy, had tried to cancel him somewhere in Lower Manhattan. The Secret Service had helped rescue Citizen Sidel. It was an American fairy tale, and Isaac was only one more Indian fighter. He could have been a native of Texas or Louisiana and Mississippi.

"Your Honor," the Mississippians said, looking at the Indian fighter's torn tie. "Are you all right?"

"Fit as a donkey," Isaac said, and the Mississippians laughed.

Reporters hovered around him, with a brace of microphones.

"Mr. Sidel, Mr. Sidel, is there a war inside your police department?"

"Not that I know of," Isaac said. He couldn't accuse an entire precinct. The convention would panic, run to another town. All he could do was smile in front of the cameras and microphones. "Had a little tussle with the bad guys, that's all."

"But who are the bad guys?"

"I'm not a cop," Isaac said. "You wouldn't want me to prejudice a criminal investigation."

Grossvogel would self-destruct like some musclebound toy. His rabbis would desert him soon enough. They couldn't afford to have Citizen Sidel nosing around on national TV.

"Is Captain Knight innocent, sir?"

"Lads," he said to the men and women with microphones, "he hasn't been arraigned yet. Give him a chance."

And he pulled away from the reporters. He'd never understand what had happened between father and son. He could have been there with his own television camera. He would have captured nothing. Family warfare was too fucking intimate for instant replay. Like a hammer in the heart. He could only mourn young Doug *and* his dad.

A huge, kicking donkey flashed onto the electronic signboard under the Garden's dome. The donkey's legs were everywhere. Smashing Republicans, Isaac presumed. The donkey disappeared . . . and different particles of a face emerged on the board. A cheek, a mouth, an eye, until conventioneers recognized the traces of Isaac Sidel. With a Glock in his hand. The Garden began to cheer. There was a kind of gleeful pandemonium. The Democrats had found their hero in the mean streets of Manhattan. The balloting could begin.

2

He couldn't even write his own acceptance speech. Isaac wanted to talk about poverty and drugs, and the dying borough of the Bronx. But Timmy wouldn't let him.

"We have a candidate to sell. You're a known quantity, the mayor of New York. But Michael is still in the woods."

The new czar of baseball didn't carry a Glock in his pants, like Isaac did.

"Kid," Tim said, "you'll take the back seat. We have to groom Michael, paste a lot of feathers on him. You'll talk about Michael, not about yourself and the City's problems."

"Jesus, Tim, don't we have a platform?"

"Not on prime time," said Tim Seligman. "No ideas, Isaac. Just stories. You'll reminisce, remind America how you fathered J."

"I didn't father him. I kept him out of jail when he was a student radical."

"But you'll soften the blow. Half the world was rebelling in sixty-eight. You won't mention that Michael was a Maoist. He was championing student rights at Columbia, against a harsh administration. He's a doer. He doesn't stand still."

"I paint a portrait, huh?"

"Perfect. You hit the nail right on the nose. A portrait, Isaac, with a lot of white space. We appeal to America's imagination."

"Create Michael, spin him out of cotton candy."

"Isaac, whatever we do, we make it sweet."

Isaac wanted to strangle Tim, or blow his brains out. He was already sick of being a Democrat, of luring the convention to *his* town.

He could resign, shove out all the delegates, but his own people would consider him a big baby. What right did he have to cry. There wasn't a vacant room in Manhattan. The Dems had brought a week of prosperity. But he couldn't mouth the words of Tim Seligman's speech writers. "Our future President is a family man."

Clarice, J.'s wife, was having an affair with one of Isaac's detectives, Bernardo Dublin. And who knows how many mistresses J. had? He and Clarice had plotted to pull millions out of the Bronx with a real-estate scam. And the mayor had to be mum, couldn't accuse the Party's warhorse. But how could Isaac sing the Democratic song? "He's as American as baseball, and almost as tough. J. Michael Storm."

J. had tried to have Clarice killed, so he could collect insurance money. He'd hired Bernardo Dublin, Isaac's detective, who was also a thug. But it was like Shakespeare in Isaac's Manhattan. Bernardo and Clarice fell in love. And Clarice would only become Michael's First Lady if she could bring

Bernardo along to the White House as her bodyguard. It was a fucking sitcom, a soap opera for idiots, and Isaac had to join the ride.

He returned to Gracie Mansion after his sit-down with Tim. He had to get away from the convention floor. Delegates were ripping off pieces of his shirt. He met with Mississippi for half an hour. The whole delegation wanted to handle Isaac's Glock.

But he wasn't alone at his mansion. Michael's daughter, Marianna Storm, was baking cookies in the kitchen.

"Marianna, shouldn't you be with your mom and dad?"

"And smile at a million photographers? I'd rather hide with you."

"But it's politics. The Dems will eat me alive if they ever find out."

"We won't tell them, will we, Mr. Mayor?" And she began to feed him butterscotch cookies. All the bitter slag of the convention fell off with the first bite. He'd kill for one of Marianna's cookies. He'd have hired her as his chef, but not even Isaac could get Marianna working papers. She was only twelve.

Seligman was counting on her green-eyed beauty to mask the coldness between Clarice and J. Images of Marianna had begun to invade America's networks and magazines. *Newsweek* called her the most photogenic little lady on the planet. She couldn't go into the street without men and women gawking at her. And so she hid out at Gracie Mansion with Isaac Sidel.

"Darling," she said, flirting with the mayor and poking fun at him. "I read your speech . . . it stinks."

"I know it stinks. But Seligman shackled me with it."

"You can't say all those things about my father. They're lies."

"And what's my choice? They'll crucify me."

"Isaac," she said, "be a man. You're the mayor. And the next vice-president. You don't have to eat crumbs off Tim Seligman's plate . . . I'll help you rewrite the speech."

"I'm scared," Isaac said. "I can handle gangsters and cops, but not sharks like Tim."

"You'll turn him into a pussycat. I promise. Just give me a pencil."

She had more brains than Isaac and a better writing style. She began to scribble in the margins, cross out every other line, while Isaac gobbled a whole fortune of butterscotch cookies.

"I'm tired," she said, after an hour.

Isaac barked at his chauffeur. "Mullins, come here."

"Boss, you want me to drive the little lady?"

"I'm not a little lady," Marianna said. "And I'm not going to live in the White House with Mama." She kissed Isaac on the mouth. "I hope you like your speech."

His hands were trembling. He could barely clutch the pages of his speech. Marianna wouldn't have poisoned him with her cookies, but he had a bellyache and he was going blind. He couldn't read a word Marianna had written. All the lines had liquified.

He fell asleep in his chair. He dreamt of a sailor on a ship. But the ship was stationary. It didn't move. The sailor was clutching a red harpoon. He had no eyes. He wore a helmet with a strange antenna on top, like the leaves of a rusted flower. The fish he attacked had orange mouths and patches of color, like a quilt. They were locked in some design, as stationary as the eyeless sailor and his ship. Isaac had become a genius in his sleep, could dredge up images, dream of paintings on a wall, a masterpiece. Ah, if people could only die with such perfection.

But he heard a cruel ring, and he had to rouse himself. He had a telephone in his fist.

"Isaac?"

He recognized the voice of Clarice. He'd have to get used to campaigning with Michael's First Lady. "What's wrong?"

"Marianna's missing."

"What the hell do you mean? I sent her home with Mullins."

"She was with you?"

"It's no secret. She has the run of the house. She likes to bake cookies."

"Past midnight?"

"It wasn't even dinnertime . . . she should have gotten to Sutton Place before dark."

"Then you're an idiot. She never got to Sutton Place. Find my daughter, or I'll tear your teeth out," she said, talking like Sidel.

The Big Guy had been cheated, tricked by his own dream. The eyeless sailor was Sidel himself, hunting in the dark with a red harpoon. He paged his chauffeur. But Mullins never called back. And Isaac didn't have a clue, not one idea where to look for Marianna Storm. He blinked. Somebody was sitting across from him in his own living room. The Big Guy groaned. It was Martin Boyle.

— 25 —

"Who let you in? This house is a fortress. I'm protected day and night."

"Mr. President," Boyle said, clutching a ring of skeleton keys. "I went to housebreaking school."

"I told you a million times. Don't call me Mr. President."

"I apologize, sir. But facts are facts. The Republicans are frightened of you, not J. Michael Storm. They'll drive right over him. But you're a wall."

"You still haven't told me what the hell you're doing here. Can't I have a little privacy?"

"Not when you're on the Democratic ticket. I eat with you, I sleep with you. I'm Crazy Glue."

"That's my reward," Isaac said. "*Crazy Glue*. Marianna Storm is missing."

"I'm aware of that, sir. She's as naughty as you are. She ducked out on Joe, went right off the screen."

"Who's Joe?"

"One of us, sir."

"Marianna has her own Secret Service man?"

"It's mandatory, sir."

"She's twelve years old, for Christ's sake. A little girl."

"She's still the daughter of a possible President."

"Who kidnapped her? Arafat? The Colombians? Fidel?"

"I'd start closer to home. Wouldn't rule out the Republican National Committee or the Democrats themselves. They're always goosing each other. Why not grab Michael's daughter? There's a lot of embarrassment value to be gained . . . by both parties."

"Son of a bitch," Isaac said.

"I could be wrong. You have lots of enemies, Mr. President."

"We can't sit here, Boyle. Who'll help us solve this case?"

"We don't need help. You have enough clout. The Citizen could get anyone he wants on the line. Should we try the Bureau?"

"The Bureau hates my guts. I'm in love with their secret agent, Margaret Tolstoy."

"She's cute. She runs around Washington in a wig."

"You know Margaret?"

"I had coffee with her once at the White House. She came with some foreign gentleman. He had lots of medals on his chest."

"Margaret visits the White House?"

"The Prez loves to give soirees."

"Did she ever come with the Bull?"

"No, sir. The Prez doesn't like to socialize with Bull Latham."

"That's a pity. Latham can't be seen in public with his master spy."

"Should I get him on the phone, sir?"

"Bull wouldn't talk to me."

"Wanna bet? You're the hottest guy in the country."

"It's three A.M., Boyle."

"He'll take the call."

Boyle grabbed Isaac's telephone, got the Bureau's switchboard on the line. "Bull Latham, please . . . you'll have to wake him. It's Isaac Sidel."

Boyle winked at Isaac and handed him the phone. Isaac's knees were shaking. Bull Latham was a linebacker with the

Dallas Cowboys who went to law school and joined the FBI. He didn't like to sit behind a desk. Latham would rush into the line of fire with his own men. He'd get into fistfights, tackle Mafia chieftains. He ran the FBI like a football team.

"Mr. Director?" Isaac whispered into the wire.

"Call me Bull . . . what can I do for you, Sidel?"

Isaac wanted to sing Margaret Tolstoy's name, but he didn't dare. No one questioned the linebacker about his own business.

"I have a problem, Bull . . . J. Michael's daughter is missing."

"Kind of disappeared after she left your mansion, isn't that right?"

"Yes, Bull. And I was wondering if . . ."

"I could have sixty agents at your door in half an hour, Sidel, but you wouldn't appreciate that much firepower. And you can't afford the publicity . . . not until you and Michael have made your speeches. How can Michael address the convention without his darling daughter at his side? It's a bit of a dilemma. Wouldn't you say so, Sidel?"

"Who took Marianna away from me?"

"Not us," Bull said, "not the Bureau . . . can we talk policeman to policeman? It's a local matter, Sidel. Your own cops stole Marianna Storm."

"I don't believe it."

"Then I've failed you. But I'll have to say good-bye. Can't function without my beauty sleep."

The Big Guy prowled his own living room. "My cops are working for the Republican National Committee?" The sailor with the red harpoon flashed in front of his eyes. But Sidel wasn't napping on his feet. He was having one of his revelations, interpreting his own dreams. Isaac realized the particular fish he had to harpoon.

"Boyle, get your hat. We're going places."

"I wasn't wearing a hat, sir."

"Then imagine one, because we'll have to depend on our thinking caps."

And the two hatless hatters crept out of Gracie Mansion in the middle of the night.

They didn't get very far. A bunch of cops met Isaac and his Secret Service man outside the gate. With them was Barton Grossvogel, wearing a whistle and white gloves. He'd come to Isaac in his parade uniform, his fists as fat as a man's head.

"Mr. Mayor, can I talk to you without your shadow?"

"Bart," Isaac said, "meet Martin Boyle."

"We've already met, haven't we, Boyle?"

"Where?" Isaac asked, like a sullen boy. Everyone seemed to know Sidel's business better than Sidel.

"At the White House," Grossvogel said, "where do you think? Walk with me, will ya?" He grabbed Isaac's arm and led him into the depths of Carl Schurz Park.

"You stole Michael's daughter."

"I did not."

"But you can tell me where she is."

"I have my spies, Isaac, just like you. I might be able to repatriate that little girl."

"And what do I have to do, Bart? Kiss your ass on the convention floor?"

Grossvogel smiled. "Nothing as drastic as that. You'll promise to lay off, to leave my shop alone."

"While you rule Elizabeth Street with your own jungle law."

"The statistics don't support your little theory. Murder and mayhem are down seventeen percent in my precinct."

"That's because a fucking dark prince like you can manufacture your own statistics."

"Watch your language, Mr. Mayor."

"Why are you in white gloves?"

"Didn't you know? I'm part of the honor guard at the convention. Do you like my medals, Mr. Mayor?"

"You're protected, aren't you? Is Bull Latham behind you? Or do you belong to the White House?"

"A modest captain like me? Will you cooperate? There'll be no acceptance speeches without that little girl. The convention will fall into some twilight zone. The delegates will have to stay in Manhattan forever."

"It's good for business," Isaac said. "Is she safe?"

"The darling daughter? How can I give you my guarantee?"

Isaac rushed Grossvogel in the dark, but the captain danced around him and socked Isaac in the face. The mayor fell on his ass. He dreamed of that eyeless sailor again. But the sailor had lost his harpoon. His ship was sinking. Isaac opened his eyes and looked up at Boyle.

"You're bleeding, sir."

"Of course I'm bleeding. Did you see the size of his fists? He's a weight lifter."

"Shouldn't we return to the mansion, clean you up?"

"We don't have the time. Why didn't you tell me that you knew Barton Grossvogel?"

"I'm not a mindreader, sir. We never discussed Captain Bart."

"Is that what the Prez calls him?"

"I'm not sure."

"Boyle, did the Prez ask you to spy on me?"

"That wouldn't be ethical, sir. I'm paid to protect your life."

Isaac climbed up off the grass of Carl Schurz Park. He was limping a bit. He had to lean on Martin Boyle.

He hailed a cab on East End Avenue.

"Where are we going, sir?"

"To the Garden."

"Before dawn?"

"Tim Seligman never sleeps," Isaac said.

They got to Madison Square Garden, were rushed through the gates, Isaac still limping. Policemen saluted him.

"I'm not a general," Isaac growled.

He found Tim Seligman in his tiny cockpit, under the air-conditioning ducts, where Tim could orchestrate the convention and harangue crucial delegates with a radio-phone hooked around his head. Boyle had to stay outside the cockpit. There was only room for Isaac and Tim.

"Ah, so you've surfaced again," Tim muttered. "Your mouth is bloody. Wash up."

"Not while Marianna is missing."

"Christ, man, can't you stop playing the detective? We'll get Marianna back. Who the hell would harm her? We'll be running the country in four months."

"Without me," Isaac said.

"My favorite diva," Tim said, grabbing Isaac's tie. "Behave. You're a Democrat, and you're on the ticket. You can't get off."

"You promised me Margaret Tolstoy if I went to Washington."

"You'll get Margaret," Tim said. "We're already negotiating with the FBI."

"She's sleeping with the President. And Bull Latham is the beard."

"That's preposterous."

"Bull hires some phony general on his payroll to bring her to the White House. But he's the beard. The Prez is in love with Margaret, isn't he? That's what the little kidnapping is all about. He wants to embarrass me in my own town."

Seligman plucked off his radio-phone. "It's much more complicated than that."

"But you're in cahoots with those bastards."

"I am not. The Republicans are desperate. So they're trying out a little war game."

"With the help of my own police department . . . Grossvogel grabbed Marianna. And he's the President's man."

Seligman tightened his grip on Isaac's tie. And Isaac couldn't shove him away. The mayor had been in a hundred brawls. He'd bitten off a mobster's ear, had killed a crooked policeman, but he couldn't shake Tim. He tried to punch the Party's prince, but Seligman whacked him on the side of the head. And for the second time in an hour Isaac Sidel was on his ass. He crawled out of the cockpit, while Timmy grabbed at his clothes.

"Boyle," he shouted, "get me Bull Latham on the horn."

"You can't talk to the Bull," Seligman said, but Isaac had already closed the door of the cockpit.

They got to a pay telephone. It started to ring. Isaac picked up the phone and heard Bull Latham growl at him. "Sidel, is that you?"

"No, it's Sinbad the Sailor."

"Meet me in half an hour."

"How, Bull? Should I take the angels' express to D.C.?"

"I'm at the Waldorf, Sidel. Would I leave the Democrats all alone in Manhattan, with a mayor who's lost half his marbles? . . . Come up to my room. We'll have a bit of breakfast."

3

It had once been the classiest address in the world. Cole Porter kept a suite at the Waldorf. So did General MacArthur and John Fitzgerald Kennedy. Isaac remembered a film he'd seen as a boy, *Weekend at the Waldorf*. With Lana Turner and Ginger Rogers. It was 1945, and Isaac would walk up from the Lower East Side in his Sunday suit, get past the doorman with a smile, sit in a lobby as big as a battlefield, contemplate among the mirrors and the chandeliers, dream of a very fat future, with Ginger Rogers clinging to his arm. Isaac's Ginger turned out to be Margaret Tolstoy, a Roumanian orphan who showed up at his junior high school with almond eyes. She called herself Anastasia, the lost princess with holes in her stockings, and Isaac had been chasing after her ever since . . .

He didn't want to get knocked on his ass again. Seligman and Grossvogel were like infants compared to the Bull, who was a solid six foot six, and could tackle Mafia chieftains ten at a time. He'd have to anger the Bull. Isaac wanted Marianna *and* Margaret Tolstoy.

Bull Latham didn't have a suite at the Waldorf, only a room with a couple of windows that looked out upon another world of windows called midtown Manhattan, where Isaac hated to be. He'd hide out in Harlem or among the ruins of the Lower East Side, gobble yellow rice and black beans at some hole-in-the-wall. And here he was at the Waldorf-Astoria with Bull Latham of the FBI.

Bull had prepared a breakfast table, smoked salmon, with coffee and danishes, from the Waldorf's kitchen. He had blond hair and wore a paisley robe for breakfast. His fingers seemed fragile for a linebacker. He didn't have Captain Bart's fat fists.

They sat across from each other. "Is the salmon good, Sidel?"

"Delicious," Isaac mumbled with a packed mouth.

"It was flown in this morning from Nova Scotia . . ."

"The Waldorf can't resist you," Isaac said. "You played for the Cowboys."

"You're anxious about Margaret Tolstoy."

"I don't like being fucked by the FBI. You're her beard, aren't you, Bull?"

"Can you think of a better one?" Bull said, biting into his danish.

"How did it happen?"

"It was an accident, a fluke."

"She just waltzed into the White House, huh? Some fluke."

"The Prez saw her picture and he went apeshit, had to meet Margaret."

"Was he searching for the Bureau's best Mata Hari?"

"I had to show him Margaret's photograph . . . she was part of his task force."

"What task force? I thought it exists only on paper, a phantom army."

"But phantoms can move."

The Prez had announced his own war against crime. It was the linchpin of his reelection campaign. A task force with a maniacal mission. Wipe out crime in America, make each inner city safe. And now Isaac realized where Barton Grossvogel fit. The President's anti-crime commissioners were using Elizabeth Street as their own little laboratory. Grossvogel had climbed aboard the President's ship. And all the pirate-cops at his precinct had suddenly become pioneers in the Prez's "great urban struggle." It sickened Isaac.

"And where was Margaret operating?"

"Downtown D.C."

"A hop away from the White House . . . is that prick of a president ever going to give Margaret back to me?"

"He'd rather lose the election."

"I don't blame him," Isaac said. "The man's in love . . . I blame you, Bull. Margaret was mine, and you tossed her at the Prez. It was Timmy's idea, wasn't it? Hook the Prez on one of the government's whores, compromise him, cut him off at the legs while Tim keeps me dangling. Isaac Sidel and the Prez in love with the same woman. You're gambling that the Democrats will win, or you wouldn't have gotten in bed with Tim Seligman."

Bull finished his danish and smiled. "I'm FBI," he said. "I can't afford to go to bed with politicians."

"You made your deal, Bull. Timmy's promised to keep you on after the election. But you'll have to deal with me. Because I'll break Tim soon as I can. I'll shove him into the corner like a doll. He'll sit for eternity . . . where's Marianna Storm?"

"Relax. Tim will rescue her at the last minute."

"What has he promised Captain Bart? Is he going to make that thief your deputy director? I'd like a list of Bart's safe houses, all the rotten holes where he might store Marianna."

"Sidel, you'll be searching for a week. Bart isn't a dummy. You want Marianna, follow your nose."

"What the fuck does that mean?"

"Your nose, Sidel. Pay attention to Seligman's stink."

4

*S*eligman's stink.

Isaac wore a false nose at the convention, looked like Sherlock Holmes playing Shylock. He'd stolen the badge of a Texas delegate, pinned it to his chest, hid his eyes under a baseball cap. He watched Tim's cockpit, but Seligman didn't stir.

Isaac waited all morning. Finally the cockpit opened, and Tim emerged in a seersucker suit and a straw hat, like a bumpkin. Isaac understood. The prince of the Party was wearing his own disguise.

"Timmy," one of his aides barked, "I can't find the Citizen."

"Sidel? He's turned into a ghost."

"But who'll deliver his speech?"

"Another ghost."

Seligman left the Garden in his straw hat, and that ghost, Isaac Sidel, figured a stretch limo would pick him up, or one of Grossvogel's police cars, and drive him to the kidnappers' den. But Timmy marched toward the Hudson River, singing to himself. Isaac wasn't near enough to catch the tune. The prince of the Party should have been choreographing Michael's appearance at the Garden, not strolling in a straw hat.

Isaac watched Timmy go into a waterfront hotel. "Grand," the Big Guy muttered to himself and performed a jig in the street. Now he'd get Marianna back. The bums on Eleventh Avenue thought he was cracked until they realized it was the mayor in one of his masks.

"Isaac," they shouted, "talk to us."

"Shut up. Can't you see? I'm on a case."

He charged into the hotel with his Glock. The desk clerk peed in his pants when he saw the hurricane in Isaac's eyes.

"Where's the little girl?"

"Girl?"

"Don't get cute. I'll dynamite your lousy hotel. Where's the young lady?"

"In room nine."

"How many mothers are guarding her?"

"Mothers?" the clerk said. "There's only one man."

"Does he have a gun?"

"Yes." The clerk was still hysterical. "No . . . maybe."

"If there's a scratch on Marianna's body, a single mark, I'll come downstairs and put your hair on fire. Are you reading me? What's your name?"

"Milton."

Isaac tore out the wires of the hotel's ancient switchboard. "Milton, what will you do while I'm upstairs?"

"Pray," the clerk said.

"That's not good enough. You'll crawl under your desk and hide there. Understand?"

Milton disappeared under his desk, and Isaac went up to room number nine. He didn't knock. He didn't care about keys. He broke the door down with a shove of his shoulder. "Marianna," he screamed, "I'm coming."

It was a room with disgusting, dirty wallpaper. Tim Seligman was lying in bed with a gal from the Ohio delegation who'd kissed Sidel the day the Democrats had come to town. There was no Marianna Storm. The prince had taken time out for a bit of romance. Isaac was tempted to pull off his false nose, but the gal with Tim controlled the entire Ohio delegation.

"You can have my wallet," Timmy said.

"More," Isaac said. He wanted to scare the life out of Tim. "Are you Seligman, the big Democrat?"

"I am."

"And your girlfriend's another Democrat?"

"She isn't my girlfriend. We're—"

"I hate Democrats."

"Who sent you?" Timmy asked.

"The wind, the rain . . ."

The Ohio delegate hid behind Timmy's back. It upset Isaac to see her suffer. "Timmy, it's gone too far, the President's tricks."

"Shirl," Tim said, "this man isn't from the President. He's a local hood."

"He busts in here. He pronounces your name."

"We're in the papers, Shirl. We're on the tube. The hotel must have hired him."

He handed Isaac a thick wad of traveler's checks.

Isaac tore up the checks. The prince started to shake, and Isaac walked out of the room. He cursed himself. The Bull had sent him barking at the moon. He couldn't find Marianna with or without Seligman's stink.

He returned to the Garden, bumped into his chauffeur. He had to shake Mullins, whisper in his ear. "It's me. Where the fuck have you been?"

"I don't know, boss. Somebody cracked me on the head while I was walking out of Gracie with the little girl."

"And you just woke up and wandered into the Garden?"

"They put me in a cellar."

"With Marianna Storm?"

"She wasn't there, boss. They were kind to me. They let me have my heart medicine."

"Think, Mullins. Were you in the dungeon at Elizabeth Street?"

"It was too dark to tell."

"And who chauffeured you here? The captain's own cops?"

"They could have been cops, boss, but they weren't wearing uniforms. I didn't recognize any of them. They looked very clean."

"Clean," Isaac said, "very clean."

The Big Guy went up to Gracie without his driver. There was an aroma in the mansion that lightened his mood. He followed that aroma into the kitchen like a happy dog. Marianna was baking a new batch of butterscotch cookies. She wagged her head at him. "Take off that stupid nose."

"Marianna, did the bad guys let you go?"

"What bad guys?"

"The ones who grabbed you outside the mansion with Mullins."

"I don't remember. I had a dream. I was with a sailor on a ship."

"Did he have a red harpoon?"

"I think so."

Isaac laughed at the picture of Marianna and himself. A couple of twins dreaming in chorus.

"What did he catch with the harpoon?"

"Junk," Marianna said. "Nothing but junk. A rusty badge. An old shoe."

"And then what happened?"

"I opened my eyes . . . and I was on a bench in Carl Schurz Park. So I came here."

They'd chloroformed her, put a rag in her mouth, slipped her into Elizabeth Street, and then carried her back up to Isaac's domain.

"Marianna, did you call your mom?"

"Why should I? I only had a nap."

"Some nap." He called Clarice. He'd have to lie like Sinbad the Sailor.

"Found her," he said. "It's my fault. She fell asleep in one of the bedrooms. Clarice, I swear. I didn't even know she was in the house."

"You son of a bitch," Clarice said, "wait until you're vice-president. J. will send you to Siberia."

Marianna grabbed the phone. "Mother, stop picking on

Isaac . . . I'm fine. I don't have to come home. Isaac will bring me to the convention."

Marianna started to undress. Isaac panicked, found her a robe. She took a bath while the Big Guy's maid washed and ironed Marianna's clothes. He crept upstairs, stood in front of the mirror, frightened of his own face. He was a madman with a harpoon. Sinbad the Sailor. He put on another suit from Milan and went back down to Marianna, who looked like an angel in her ironed clothes.

"Darling," she said, "don't forget your speech."

They were like royalty. Isaac and Marianna walked arm in arm, and had their own mysterious glow under the Garden lights. The Democratic donkey flashed onto the electric sign-board over their heads. Then an image of Marianna displaced the donkey. She'd become the Democrats' little darling, and Isaac was her escort, him with the battered face.

They marched to the podium, sat among Party people. Clarice was already chafing. Her own daughter had outclassed her on the night of J. Michael's acceptance speech. The magnificent décolleté of her dress was nothing compared to the grace of a twelve-year-old girl.

The cameras were on Isaac and the Garden's little first lady. But the Big Guy wasn't thinking of his Democratic future. He saw Bull Latham in the crowd, among the crisscrossed sign-boards of each delegation. He crept off the podium and followed Bull into the men's room. As soon as Bull entered one of the toilet stalls, Isaac banged the door against him, and climbed on the Bull's back.

"You kidnapped Marianna. Captain Bart was only your accomplice. It was your men who brought Marianna back to the Garden."

"You're crazy, Sidel. I had to act once Bart grabbed the girl. I couldn't stay out of the loop. I negotiated for Tim . . . and get the fuck off my back."

Isaac bit the Bull's ear, and Latham ran with him across the men's room like a linebacker.

"What did you promise Bart?"

Bull knocked Isaac against the wall. A mirror smashed. The Big Guy slumped to the floor. His suit had ripped at the shoulder. Bull kicked him once and was about to walk away. "I promised him the world, if you'd like to know."

Isaac wasn't finished. He tackled Bull Latham, who twisted around and kept smashing Isaac with his elbows. The Big Guy lost a tooth. He had blood on his shirt. He blinked and blinked, but he couldn't see the Bull. Then an angel appeared in the men's room. Martin Boyle. Boyle was holding Isaac's Glock against the Bull's cheek.

"You wouldn't shoot," the Bull said. "I'm FBI."

"I might," Boyle said, "if you had homicide on your mind. Let the Citizen go."

Bull walked inside the stall, and Boyle helped Isaac to his feet.

"Martin," Isaac said, "I'm blind. I can't see a fucking thing."

"It will pass, Mr. President. He hit you pretty hard."

Boyle shoved the Glock back inside Isaac's pants, walked him out of the men's room and onto the podium, with cameras flicking in his face. He wanted to find his seat, but Tim grabbed his arm and shoved him toward the microphone, hissing into his back. "Damn you, it's time for your speech."

Ah, he hadn't looked at Marianna's version. He started to pat his pockets. He'd lost his speech in the men's room. It didn't matter. He'd sing a mayor's song. "I'm Sinbad," he said, "and I accept my Party's nomination," before he swooned and fell off the podium, into the arms of his Secret Service man.

The Democrats climbed ten points in the polls. They had a fighter on their team who warred with the FBI and delivered the shortest acceptance speech in American history.

He was rushed to Roosevelt Hospital, slept with a tube in his arm. Marianna visited him in the morning, kissed him on the forehead. "Darling," she said, "Mother wants to disown me. But I thought you were wonderful. Who would ever dare campaign against Sinbad the Sailor?"

Isaac closed his eyes. He was content. His body curled over. He started to dream. Sinbad had his red harpoon. He dredged a monster with a humped back out of the sea. It wasn't a shark or a baby whale. Isaac's catch had human eyes. His mouth shaped a scream.

"Shhh. I won't harm you."

It was Daniella Grossvogel. She'd come to Isaac in a blue skirt, with blood-red roses in her hand.

"Did your father send you?" Isaac asked.

"No, Mr. Mayor. Dad would murder me if he knew I was here. But I had to come. I betrayed you."

"Professor Grossvogel, you're not my bride."

"It's worse than that."

"Ah," Isaac sang, with the only humor he could summon from his hospital bed. "Did you send that gangster in orange pants after me? Babel's gangster. What's his name? Benya Krik. The guy who owns Odessa's Lower East Side."

"I wish it were Benya Krik," Daniella said. "You would have got along with him."

"He's only fiction," Isaac had to mutter.

"Sometimes fiction can leap off the page."

"But can it govern seven million souls? Ah, I'm getting philosophical. Forgive me, Daniella."

"I'm the one who has to beg forgiveness. I betrayed you. I minded Marianna Storm for Dad. I was her babysitter."

"I don't get it."

"Dad brought her to me, carried her in his arms. She was in quite a heavy sleep, almost like a coma. And he didn't want to leave Michael's girl with his own ruffians at the station-house. So I was elected, Mr. Mayor."

"But you could have phoned me."

"It was too dangerous. I wasn't alone. Dad's policemen were in the other room."

"And why are you telling me now?"

"I'm ashamed," she said. "I'm a criminal, like Dad and young Doug. I belong to Dad's crime school."

"Nah," Isaac said, "you had to protect the little girl. She was safe with you. I'm the one who ought to be grateful. You should have married Dougy, eloped with him, pulled him away from Elizabeth Street."

"I couldn't," she said. "Elizabeth Street had become his opium den. He liked to imagine himself as Benya Krik."

"Daniella, did he wear orange pants?"

"Most of the time. But he wasn't Benya. Benya wouldn't have worked for Barton Grossvogel. Benya didn't like police stations."

"Maybe some magician could bring him back alive. I liked the kid. He was a good cop."

"Before my father got to him."

"It's not so simple. The White House was running Elizabeth Street. I just found out. Elizabeth Street was part of the President's phantom commission. Can you imagine? Barton Grossvogel doing hits for the United States."

"That's how Dad sucked Dougy in so deep. It was like a religious order. The President's band of criminal knights. But Dougy never got rich. He borrowed from Dad, gave all his money to an assortment of lowlifes."

"Until his own father shot him dead."

"Don't believe it. Captain Knight didn't kill Dougy."

"Then who did?"

"I'm not sure," Daniella said. "Dad might have ordered his execution, but he loves me in his own stupid way. And he wouldn't have deprived his crippled daughter of a husband."

"Then how the hell did Dougy die?"

Daniella shrugged her shoulders. "It's a mystery, Mr. Mayor." She left the roses on Isaac's bed and was gone before the invalid could thank her or say good-bye.

Part Two

5

He had the little first lady all to himself. The Democrats didn't want Marianna on the same bus with Clarice. And they didn't want Sidel. Seligman and his spin doctors couldn't capitalize on Sidel's popularity without hurting Michael. And so they developed a strategy to contain Isaac, keep him out of Michael's hair.

He wouldn't tour with Michael and Clarice. He would stick to his mansion, or make little forages into the heartland.

He went up to Peekskill with Marianna Storm. He wasn't on a Democratic mission. Isaac had to play Marianna's beard. She was in love with Angel Carpenteros, aka Alyosha, a twelve-year-old artist and police spy who belonged to the Latin Jokers, the biggest and baddest gang of the Bronx. Alyosha had drawn murals on the walls of Featherbed Lane, celebrating the gang's fallen heroes, heroes he himself had helped to trap. Isaac couldn't figure out the politics of a Bronx gang. Alyosha had been caught between the cops and the Bronx's natural chaos. Isaac himself had introduced the muralist to Marianna at a meeting of Merlin (one of his cockeyed schemes, a cultural enrichment program), and the two kids fell in love, Marianna Storm of Sutton Place South and Angel Carpenteros, address unknown. Isaac had to tuck Alyosha away at a posh juvenile facility in Peekskill, where the Latin Jokers couldn't get to him and peel off his skin for having betrayed the gang.

"Darling," Marianna said, "let's hide Alyosha in your mansion. I'm lonely without him."

"Wouldn't I hide him if I could? Reporters are all over the place. And if they run into Alyosha? Think of the headlines. Candidate's daughter romances local artist-hoodlum-priest."

"He isn't a hoodlum."

"But the press will call him that. And the Jokers will find him. He wouldn't last a week."

The Big Guy was guilty as hell. He hated institutions. But Peekskill Manor had all the trappings of a country club, even if it was locked behind a gate with wires that could produce a terrible shock. There was plenty of privacy within the manor walls, where Marianna and the muralist could kiss and stroll, with Isaac a hundred feet behind them. The Big Guy was embarrassed. He'd never seen such hunger in two twelve-year-olds. Romeo and Juliet were like kindergartners compared to them.

"Boss," Alyosha said, "do you have to trail us? I'm glad to see you. But enough is enough. We're Merliners. We have things to discuss."

"I'm responsible," the Big Guy said.

Marianna hissed at him. "Uncle Isaac, go away. Get lost."

And Isaac had to sit on a bench with his Secret Service man and Marianna's. "You're not to breathe a word," he barked because he had no other audience at Peekskill Manor. "Alyosha doesn't exist. I don't want him mentioned in any briefs . . . or gossip among you guys."

"We won't upset the lovebirds," said Marianna's Secret Service man, Joe Montaigne, a sharpshooter from Missouri.

"They're not lovebirds," Isaac said. "They're gifted children, Merliners—"

"Who like to kiss."

"You're not supposed to notice that," Isaac said to Joe Montaigne.

"Then how can we protect them?"

"Look again, Montaigne. This manor is a closed world."

"Any little acrobat can scale a wall . . . we have to watch them kiss."

Marianna and her muralist returned in half an hour with swollen eyes and lips.

"Uncle," Alyosha said, "I want to marry her."

"Keep quiet. There's a price on your head."

"I'll run away from here. Me and Marianna can't live apart."

"Grand," Isaac said. They could move into the Democratic caravan, with Clarice and her "bodyguard," Bernardo Dublin. It was Bernardo who'd destroyed half the Latin Jokers, even though Bernardo had once been a Joker himself. Isaac had recruited him right out of the gang, sent him to the Police Academy, taught him a policeman's tricks. Isaac was responsible for Bernardo and Alyosha and the dead gangs of the Bronx. The children Alyosha had painted in his murals were casualties of Isaac's war. The Big Guy had decimated a borough in his zeal to clean up the Bronx. He was some kind of Oliver Cromwell.

"Darling," Marianna said, "you'll have to give Alyosha to me . . . I won't step inside the White House without him."

"Would you both like the Lincoln Bedroom?"

"No," Alyosha said. "It's filled with ghosts."

"Marianna, it would take a miracle to arrange the marriage of two twelve-year-olds, but even if I could, I'd only be hastening Alyosha's death. The Jokers would get to him."

"I'll use another name," Alyosha said.

"Homey, you have no other name."

And Isaac whisked Marianna away from Peekskill before she could kiss Alyosha again. She'd become Isaac's houseguest while Clarice and Michael were on the road. She bossed the cooks and maids around, prepared hard-boiled eggs for Isaac in the morning, ironed his summer suits, called Peekskill every night, punished the mayor with a fat phone bill. But the Big Guy loved having her around. It eased the ache of losing Margaret Tolstoy, knowing she was in the President's arms. He'd glut himself with Marianna's cookies and produce a prodigious bellyache.

He couldn't stop thinking of Captain Knight and his dead son. A funny thing had already happened. The grand jury wouldn't hand down a bill of indictment. Captain Doug was sent home from his monk's cell at Criminal Courts. Grossvogel and his men swore that young Doug had been drinking and cursing at Elizabeth Street, talked of shooting his dad, stealing money from his mom. It was a little too neat a scenario. A father shoots his son in self-defense. The captain would have wrestled Dougy's gun away. Isaac rode out to Pineapple Street, but neither the captain nor his wife would see him.

Isaac had to shout through the door. "Doug, will you speak to me, for Christ's sake? I could break in, you know. I could pick your locks."

But the Big Guy didn't do a thing. And the next day Doug disappeared from Brooklyn Heights, moved out to Scottsdale, Arizona, with his wife, to live in the land of perpetual sun. Isaac had nothing against Scottsdale. He could have retired there himself, among the cactus plants, and a Howard Johnson's that served a seven-course meal. He could have lectured at Arizona State, become an adjunct professor of criminal justice, even an honorary sheriff, but Captain Doug was Brooklyn-born, proud of Pineapple Street. He might have played golf in Scottsdale, but he'd never have given up his native ground. Isaac had served with Doug when he was the Commish, had pinned medals on him. Doug didn't scare. But somebody had chased him out of Brooklyn.

Isaac neglected Marianna, forgot to campaign. He wandered around Elizabeth Street, searching for some imaginary creature in orange pants. What had Daniella said, with her fistful of blood-black roses? Sometimes fiction can leap off the page. But nothing leaped. There were no Benya Kriks in Isaac's back yard.

A rage built in him. He was being used. He'd become the Democratic bulldog who had to sit with a rope around his neck when he wanted to run to D.C., find Margaret Tolstoy, and grab her away from the President. But he would have ruined the show, toppled that crazy house of American politics. Jack Kennedy had had a dozen mistresses, shared one or two with the Maf, another with his own brother Bob, but no previous president had battled the mayor of New York over the rights to a gorgeous double agent who was developing varicose veins.

He couldn't trust Boyle or Joe Montaigne. These were the President's men, even if they'd swallow bullets or bombs for Isaac. But he could trust a Merliner, like Marianna Storm.

"Darling," he said, "I need a pair of orange pants."

"That's ridiculous. Orange pants. The country will laugh. And you won't get elected. Not that I'd mind. I prefer Gracie Mansion to the White House."

"Don't argue," he said. "I'm on an errand. And that errand calls for orange pants."

He could have gone to the barrels of Orchard Street. But he didn't want peddlers to know his business. Marianna got to work with the maids. They didn't have to seek fresh material. They tore apart an old curtain and constructed a pair of orange pants. These pants had a magical pull. Isaac felt magnificent in them, like a gangster from the lush ghetto streets of Odessa. He had a makeup kit in his bedroom, a smattering of old clothes for his many disguises. He painted his eyebrows black. Benya Krik had to be a younger man than Sidel. He wore a red scarf, with a seaman's cap on his balding pate. And then he ducked out of the mansion, fled to *his* Maldavanka, the badlands near Elizabeth Street.

Nothing happened.

He pointed himself like a compass and went deeper into the badlands. He wasn't campaigning now. He wasn't Sidel or

Sinbad the Sailor. He was hiking in his orange pants. His painted eyebrows began to melt. He hadn't considered the sun. Did he look like some drag queen?

A little boy came up to him, handed Isaac a rotting flower. "El Señor," the boy said.

Grandmothers and little girls bowed to him. An old man gave him a crumpled dollar bill, not as tribute, but as some special totem. More and more people gave him crumpled dollar bills.

He was having the time of his life until Elizabeth Street caught up with him, discovered his charade. Captain Bart stepped out of a patrol car.

"What the fuck are you doing, Sidel?"

"I'm not sure. But it's my guess that some of the citizens are mistaking me for young Doug."

"Dougy's dead."

"Then what are those crumpled bills all about?"

"Get into the car, will ya, Sidel? Or do we have to drag you in plain daylight?"

Isaac got into the car. Grossvogel wiped the rivulets of black paint from Isaac's cheeks with a big handkerchief.

"Shall we have our own true confessions, huh, Mr. Mayor? Dougy was out of his mind. He dreamt he was a character in a book."

"Benya Krik."

"I don't care about the details. He'd gone insane. That was enough. He was protecting the little people."

"And they thanked him with crumpled dollar bills."

"Evidently. But he didn't collect enough. He was robbing merchants and Mafia button men, giving all his loot to dope addicts and skels who lived on the roofs . . . like the whole precinct was his patrimony, his private estate."

"Maldavanka," Isaac mumbled.

"Will ya listen to me? He robbed from other cops, from his own fucking captain. I wanted to psycho him out, but it would have left a scar on my ship. So I talked to his dad, I summoned Captain Knight to Elizabeth Street for a chat, and that son of a bitch blamed me, said I was corrupting Doug Jr., teaching him how to steal. Jesus, man, didn't we drive half the Mafia out?"

"With money from the White House and Bull Latham."

"The Bureau can spend millions, but I can't . . . the dons are in jail. And the Chinese gangs have moved out to Queens. Sidel, I run a quiet ship."

"Too quiet. You shouldn't have grabbed Marianna, drugged a little girl."

"Ah, Daniella's been talking to you, eh? Didn't I take care of the girlie? Nothing rough. She had the best babysitter in the world. My own daughter. And I returned the package, didn't I? No harm done . . . and you shouldn't go around in orange pants, Sidel. That's what pimps wear in the barrio. I'd have to arrest you for soliciting. And it would cause a scandal."

The captain produced an enormous pair of scissors from under his seat. He signaled to his men, who held Isaac down, while the captain proceeded to cut different patterns in Isaac's pants, like some inspired couturier.

"I could kill you right now. Dump you in some lot. They wouldn't find you for a month. But you're a lucky man. You have your own champion in the White House. The Prez is

awful fond of you. You're his hero. A mayor with a Glock in
his pants. He'd have to commit suicide if Michael wasn't such
a mediocre candidate. 'Can't we turn Isaac around, make him
into a Republican?' That's what the President said to me."

"He stole my woman."

"I'm not prepared to discuss the President's love life,"
Grossvogel said and continued to cut Isaac's pants.

"Are you finished, Bart?"

"Almost."

He delivered Isaac to Carl Schurz Park and socked him in
the face. "Don't ever come into my turf again."

"Your turf, Bart? I grew up on the Lower East Side."

"But you graduated to Gracie Mansion. It's healthier for
you uptown."

Isaac went through the gate in his tattered orange pants like
some medieval jester. The detectives from his own detail didn't
dare smirk at him. But Isaac felt a chill in his bones. It had
nothing to do with torn pants. He had a guest from D.C.
Margaret Tolstoy with her almond eyes, her silver hair
cropped like an army recruit. Isaac wanted to smile, but he
couldn't. She hadn't come to him out of some crazy whim, the
desire to see an old school chum. He'd been in love with a
phantom these forty years. *Anastasia*. He was gloomy again.
Margaret was the President's lady . . . and the President's man.

6

"Hello, bashful. I like your pants."

He hadn't seen her in months. She'd lived with him in Gracie as his houseguest and disappeared. Bull Latham, that son of a bitch, had sneaked her into Prague. It was Timmy's doing. Tim had prodded the Bull to get rid of Anastasia, while the Democrats groomed Isaac, prepared him for the vice-presidency. Foreign diplomats began to fall in love with Isaac's dark lady, and Tim had to pull her out of Prague.

"Came for a visit," she said. "I can't stay."

They went up to Isaac's bedroom. She undressed. Isaac peeked at her varicose veins. They were like gorgeous landmarks on her body. She shucked off Isaac's clothes. It didn't matter how artful she was. Isaac's prick was asleep. He couldn't make love to Margaret.

Should he ask her about her trips to the White House?

"I missed you," she said. "Your curly hair."

"Margaret, look again. I'm practically bald."

"Stop kidding me. You have half a forest."

He considered strangling her. He couldn't. She stared at his miserable peanut. "I'm out of practice," he said. "You shouldn't have left me like that. I wake up. You're gone."

"I'm a whore."

"That's no explanation," he said. "Tim told me about your exploits in Prague. Every diplomat in the country was under your spell."

"It's your fault. You entered politics. How could I live in a mansion with you? You're a married man."

"Means nothing. Haven't seen Kathleen in years."

He'd married the Countess Kathleen when he was just a kid. A redhead in real estate she was. She introduced Isaac to the Irish Mafia at the NYPD. They had a daughter, Marilyn the Wild, who kissed all the boys in the cellars of Marble Hill. Kathleen fled to Florida, became a millionairess, and Isaac had holes in his pockets, spent all his money on the baseball team he managed in the Police Athletic League. If the Democrats won, Isaac would be the first pauper vice-president.

"Kathleen wouldn't interfere in the election," Isaac said. "She'd never hurt me."

"Maybe. Maybe not. But there's another complication. I'm also married."

Ah, his prick started to stir. "Married to whom?"

"The Butcher of Bucharest."

"Antonescu? Jesus, you were a baby. You couldn't have been more than eleven when you married him."

"Twelve."

"Twelve's not a legal marriage."

"It was in Odessa."

Ferdinand Antonescu ruled the Black Sea during World War II, had his own little Nazi state, and managed to smuggle his bride out of Odessa in forty-four, on a Red Cross boat.

"I thought the Russians killed him."

"No. He was with a circus for a little while."

"Margaret, he must be a hundred years old."

"He's eighty-five and he has all his teeth . . . lives in Alexandria."

"How the hell did he get to Egypt?"

"Not that Alexandria. He's in a nursing home near the Potomac."

"An FBI crib," Isaac said. "That's the hold the Bureau has over you. Goddammit. You have to protect a living ghost."

"He's not a ghost. He raised me, Isaac."

"And took you into his bed."

"I was a waif. He paid for my ballet lessons."

"And took you into his bed. I'd call it fucking child abuse."

"We didn't have such fancy terms in those days. He kept me alive. I'd never have met you without Ferdinand."

"Should I go to that crib and thank him, dear?"

She slapped Isaac's face. It wasn't torture. His peanut grew. He made love to Margaret. He was just as evil as the Butcher of Bucharest. He was filled with spite.

"Who sent you? Bull Latham or the Prez?"

"Calder would skin me alive if he knew I was here. I had to dodge the Secret Service. They're with me around the clock."

"That's funny. I have the Secret Service right in this house."

"They're your Secret Service men, not Calder's."

"Aren't they part of the same stinking show? Calder Cottonwood and his band."

"Don't mock the President of the United States."

"Margaret," Isaac asked, "are you patriotic all of a sudden? What did America do but turn you into a huntress?"

"It introduced me to a gypsy schoolboy, Isaac Sidel."

"I wasn't such a gypsy," Isaac said.

"But that's what I tell the President."

"You talk about us?"

"All the time."

"The intimate details of our romance?"

"Every one. He can't go to sleep without some new adventure about us . . . Isaac, I'm his Scheherazade."

"Grand," Isaac said. He wanted to will his past away, forget the little girl with holes in her socks who destroyed the stability of Isaac's class, turned boys into beggars competing for Margaret's charms. She called herself the Princess Anastasia, royalty who'd arrived out of nowhere and was whisked back to Roumania, where she continued her schooling at a KGB kindergarten. Was she already working for the FBI? A double agent who played with dolls.

She touched Isaac's cheek. "Imbecile. Calder can't live without my stories. He's impotent."

"That's kind of you to say. I don't believe it. He's always chasing women."

"Now he chases me . . . Calder's seen a hundred urologists. They can't do a thing. But my stories soothe him. Sometimes he has a tiny erection, but it never stays."

"And I have to hear about it?"

"You love details. You could be Calder's twin."

"Does the Prez want to whack me, put a bullet in my brain?"

"Warm, darling . . . I've been hunting for a renegade cop."

"Captain Grossvogel?"

"Not Grossvogel. One of his men."

Isaac had to bite his lip. Sinbad the Sailor was a prophet on his little boat. Dougy wasn't dead.

"You're going into the Maldavanka, aren't you?"

"This isn't Odessa, darling. This isn't the Black Sea."

"Wanna bet? You're chasing a guy in orange pants."

"Benya Krik. You've been reading too many books. And don't question me, darling. You have your own Lolita in the house."

"What Lolita?"

"That cutie pie who pretends she's Clarice's daughter."

"She is Clarice's girl. Marianna Storm."

"Are you sleeping with her?"

"Margaret, she's twelve."

"I was rolling around with Uncle Ferdinand long before that."

"But I'm not Ferdinand. And Marianna's in love with a little street artist. She has her own bedroom in the mansion. And a bodyguard."

Anastasia started to dress.

"I could keep you here," Isaac muttered, "lock you in this room."

"It's been tried . . . you'd have bodies everywhere, and Bull would get mad at me."

"But Dougy doesn't deserve to die."

"You're talking riddles, Isaac. Did I say 'die'? And who's Dougy?"

"Captain Knight's boy."

"He's already dead. And I don't do miracles."

She kissed Isaac Sidel, sucked at his face, and ran away from him before he could summon the Secret Service.

7

He began to rise and rise in the polls. The Democratic Party had to get behind Sidel. What did he care if Seligman screamed? Isaac decided to go to Scottsdale with the little first lady. He wouldn't bumble around in Phoenix. He'd lecture to a couple of classes at the university, not as a candidate, but as a criminologist. He appealed to his Secret Service man. "Boyle, do a little shopping, will ya? Find me Captain Knight's address."

And he caught a flight with Martin Boyle, Marianna, and *her* Secret Service man, Joe Montaigne, charged the tickets to the Storm-Sidel Election Committee. He couldn't pretend to be some anonymous voyager. Everybody recognized Marianna. He was only her escort, a balding mayor with sideburns. People kept making pilgrimages to Marianna's window seat. Boyle found her a big red crayon, and she wrote "Affectionately, Marianna Storm" on menus and bookmarks and slips of paper.

There was a motorcade from the airport to the university. Marianna had to sit in the lap of her Secret Service man and wave at women and children who stood along the edge of the road with astonished looks.

"Bless you, Marianna. We hope you'll make it to the White House with Mr. Isaac."

A classroom couldn't hold Sidel. He had to lecture in the gym. Arizona was Republican country. The Prez was from Phoenix, had gone to Arizona State, might have played basketball in this very gym. But Isaac hadn't come to provoke President Cottonwood. He wouldn't talk partisan politics. He stood on a special platform near center court, with the little first lady beside him. Boyle started to tremble.

"We can't protect you, sir. Not under these conditions. It wasn't supposed to be a gym. There could be a sniper upstairs . . . with your name and Marianna's on a dumdum bullet."

"Stop worrying. I'll hold Marianna under my wing."

Isaac rocked on the platform, never mentioned Republicans, Democrats, and Calder Cottonwood's anti-crime commission. But the crowd hadn't forgotten Isaac's acceptance speech.

"Sinbad," students shouted at him, "Sinbad the Sailor."

"Kids," Isaac said, "I'm only a sailor in my dreams . . . but I'd love to recruit all of you, have you become policemen and policewomen. Because it's important. Not the pension and the other perks. Not the gun in your belt. Not the uniform. But the little marks of wisdom. I'd ask you to study Shakespeare, Dostoyevsky, and Chester Himes. Those are your real law books. Human laughter and pain. Not statistics," Isaac said.

Marianna crept out from under him. "I agree. I'd go to any cop school where Uncle Isaac can teach . . ."

"Sinbad," the students shouted, "Sinbad and the little first lady." They banged their feet against the floorboards, and the gym began to sway. Joe Montaigne handed Isaac a portable phone.

"Not now," Isaac barked.

"It's Tim Seligman, sir."

"I don't need that prick to punish me."

"Tim's not into punishment, sir."

Isaac grabbed the phone. "Yeah, Tim. I know. I'm in Cottonwood country, and I'd better get the hell out of there. But I have a chore to do."

"It was perfect," Seligman said. "I wasn't expecting a major policy address. Cops without guns, Shakespeare in their pockets. That we can sell."

"How did you happen to hear my speech?"

"We're not amateurs, Isaac. We had a radio hookup in the stands."

"Tim, are you microphoning me?"

Isaac tossed the telephone back to Joe Montaigne. "Next time, Joe, I can't be reached."

But the Big Guy wasn't through. He had to field questions from that storm of people in the stands. His heart pounded when he noticed Pamela Box among the students. Pam was Calder's chief of staff, a ferocious girl of thirty-five who'd stepped away from the White House to dog Michael during the campaign. She was also sleeping with the Prez, and Isaac could imagine how Margaret Tolstoy had begun to complicate her life. She was much younger than Margaret, more of a classic beauty, with blond hair and a perfect nose, but how could Pam compete with Margaret's varicose veins?

"Sidel, it's wonderful to imagine a world of educated constables, Shakespearean scholars roaming the streets with a Glock, but aren't you a bit naive? Will your scholars shoot when they have to shoot? Or will they quote Shakespeare to young hoodlums and psychopaths?"

Isaac didn't shy away from Pam.

"Perhaps my Shakespeareans will hesitate before they shoot. But that won't make them any less of a constable. Trigger-happy cops are psychopaths themselves. I'd rather have a cop who can reason with the worst criminals."

"Same old story," she shouted back. "But you can't have much compassion in a jungle."

"I'm not so sure. Kill compassion, and that's where the jungle begins."

"Then why are you wearing a Glock?"

"It's a weakness, Mrs. Box. I might not need one if I had more Shakespeare in my blood."

He whispered to Martin Boyle. "Let's move before she cuts us to pieces."

The university had arranged a lunch, but Isaac darted out of the gym with Marianna and the two Secret Service men. They had a meal at Howard Johnson's, where Isaac was served his own pot of coffee. He drank and drank.

"Darling," Marianna said, "you'll get palpitations."

"Don't henpeck me."

"She's right, sir," Boyle said. "You've had two pots."

"I have to fortify myself . . . Captain Knight's a tough cookie."

The Big Guy stepped across the street. The captain was hiding in a fancy bungalow behind Howard Johnson's. Isaac didn't even have to knock. Captain Knight came out to greet him.

"Sidel, go away."

"Can't, Doug. I think you and your little boy have been romancing me."

"Don't you speak of the dead like that."

"I wouldn't, but you see, Dougy's still alive."

The captain shoved Isaac into the bungalow, left Marianna and the Secret Service standing in the street.

The bungalow wasn't like Brooklyn; it had no charm. It must have been furnished by the FBI or the President's own people. Captain Doug and his wife were trapped inside a world of wallpaper, where some endless garden of tulips seemed about to swallow them up.

"How did you make me so quick, Mr. Vice-President?"

Isaac couldn't tell Captain Doug that his own Secret Service man, Martin Boyle, was on the case. Boyle had a magic resource: Isaac Sidel. Doors began to open the minute he invoked Isaac's name.

"Dougy's in danger," Isaac said.

"Make him stop," Sandra said.

"I'm not kidding. The Prez has his own hitter out looking for him. The best. Margaret Tolstoy."

Sandra began to laugh and cry. "Margaret Tolstoy."

"What's so funny?" Isaac had to ask.

"Margaret was working with Doug Jr.," the captain said. "They knocked off half the Mafia around Elizabeth Street."

"She was in Manhattan all this time?"

"How should I know, Mr. Vice-President? She could have shuttled between Manhattan and the President's bed."

"That's nice. But the Prez has still given her Dougy as her own special detail . . . what would I find if I opened Dougy's coffin? Some Mafia lowlife with his face shot off and his fingers missing?"

"Open all the coffins you want. Dougy was cremated last week."

"I was in the Maldavanka," Isaac said, "wearing orange pants."

"He's crazy," Sandra said.

"People mistook me for young Doug."

"Get out of my house," the captain said.

"They handed me crumpled dollar bills . . . you cut a deal with the President, didn't you? You staged Dougy's death. Dougy was supposed to become a sleeper, a hidden submarine, but he went right back into the badlands. Had he embarrassed the President, huh? Was he killing people he shouldn't have killed?"

Captain Knight tossed Isaac out on his ass.

The little first lady stood over Isaac, scrutinizing him.

"Are you hurt?"

"No," Isaac said. And he ran from Scottsdale with his entourage.

He couldn't leave Manhattan for one lousy day. Some graffiti artist had emerged in his absence, drew his picture on the walls of abandoned buildings. Isaac looked like a balding Che Guevara, without a mustache or a beard. Stories began to appear in newspapers and magazines about the mysterious artist. But it wasn't much of a riddle to Isaac or Marianna Storm. Angel Carpenteros had run away from his country-club prison. Isaac took to the sky. He had to find Angel before the Latin Jokers found him. He roamed Manhattan in his chopper, sat with Martin Boyle, looking down upon the relentless geometry of the streets.

"Boss, it's like trying to find a cockroach from another planet."

Isaac searched and searched, but he had no luck.

He went home to his mansion. Marianna grabbed at him, wouldn't bake the butterscotch cookies Sidel needed to survive. She'd become like his own little wife. The Big Guy wished the campaign would never end and he wouldn't have to give Marianna back to Michael and Clarice. He liked it when she bossed him and his servants. But she wouldn't get off the topic of Angel Carpenteros, that little Rembrandt who was making him look more and more like Guevara. Angel began drawing Isaac with a slight beard and a beret.

Seligman screamed from Party headquarters. "Find the artist, whoever he is. We can't afford him, Isaac. It's a Republican trick. The Prez is trying to turn you into a pinko."

"Well, Timmy, wasn't I the Pink Commish?"

"That was years ago," Seligman said. "And we scratched it out of your dossier."

Isaac didn't give a damn about Tim's complaints. He would only answer to Marianna Storm.

"He'll die out there," Marianna said. "He's so innocent."

Isaac didn't have the heart to tell her that Alyosha had helped destroy his own gang.

He went up into the sky again, with Boyle and Marianna beside him in bucket seats, and scoured the Bronx. But Alyosha had limited his art to Manhattan, outside Joker territory. And when he drew Isaac with a beret and a bigger beard on the walls of a warehouse close to Elizabeth Street, the Big Guy understood that Angel wasn't simply avoiding the Jokers: he was moving deeper and deeper into the city's desolation. Isaac ordered his pilot to hover near the Maldavanka. It frightened him. He could have been entering a bloodless black heart, some hole in the universe that might suck him in. He wanted to get the hell out, but Marianna insisted that they cruise.

"Uncle," she said, "I can feel him . . . he's here."

Isaac discovered a dead church in that no-man's-land between Essex and the East River. He looked for signs of Alyosha's art. But there were no images of Isaac as Guevara or Groucho Marx. The walls of the Maldavanka seemed deprived without Alyosha. The kid hadn't come to no-man's-land. And Isaac was prepared to turn back. He waved to his pilot, and that's when he saw the orange pants. A man was running amidst the debris. He had some kind of animal on his shoulder, like a balding cat, but Isaac wasn't close enough to really tell.

"Emilio," he barked at the pilot. "We're going down."

The chopper swerved into the wind and landed on a pile of rubble. "Wait here," Isaac said to Boyle and Marianna, and jumped out like some forlorn parachutist minus the silk on his back. He rushed toward the orange pants.

"Benya," Isaac muttered, and now he could recognize that bald animal; the guy in the orange pants had a huge rat curled around his neck. Doug Jr. had risen like Jesus Christ, and roamed the Maldavanka, where a man could take a rat as a pet.

"Dougy," Isaac said.

"Who sent you?"

He had stubble on his chin, but not a genuine beard.

"I like your pet."

"He's a fucking rat, and he doesn't like strangers. Who sent you?"

The rat stared at Isaac with a terrible longing in its pink eyes. It seemed more human than most of the wise guys Isaac had arrested.

"What's his name?"

"Raskolnikov," Dougy said. "But he won't talk to you."

"Ah, a philosopher, a talking rat."

"Why not? He has his own fucking language . . . who sent you?"

"I sent myself," Isaac said. "Margaret Tolstoy is coming into the badlands, and she means business."

"Let her come," Dougy said.

"Are you stupid? She hunts for the FBI."

"And sleeps with Calder Cottonwood."

"Why did you fake your own death, huh? Your dad had to leave Brooklyn on account of you."

"Did I have a choice, Mr. Mayor? I was part of the President's own task force. Margaret and me. We knocked off the Maf. But I wasn't satisfied. Landlords were getting greedy. They hiked up the rent in the worst shitholes, hired goons to beat up on tenants. I had to do something. I couldn't sit and watch. I whacked one of them, shot him in the head. I'm not sorry. But the Prez got scared. Not about the killing. Politicos might accuse his darling little task force of practicing socialism. I beat the hell out of another landlord. I started stealing from cops at the precinct. Was I supposed to let a lot of grandmas and babies starve? The cops were stealing from grocers. I took their loot away from them."

"A regular Robin Hood . . . with a Russian rat. Raskolnikov."

"Hey, don't mock him. He's sensitive."

"I'm sensitive too."

"Not for very long. Once you're elected, you'll be as big a prick as Calder. He put the pressure on Dad, through Captain Bart. They said I had to go. Margaret thought up the scheme while she was in bed with Cottonwood. He went for it. Margaret picked Dad as my executioner. First they found a skel . . ."

"And you were supposed to leave the badlands, go west somewhere. But you couldn't trade in your orange pants."

"Not while those landlords and lousy cops are still in bloom."

"But I told you. Margaret's coming."

"She's one more pistolero, Isaac. I pity her."

"I could arrest you. I have the Secret Service with me."

"I know. And Marianna Storm. They're right behind you."

Martin Boyle and the little first lady had left the chopper, and stood with Sidel. Marianna kept staring at the rat on Dougy's shoulder. And that's when Isaac heard Raskolnikov squeal like a soprano singing inside a tunnel made of tin.

Isaac understood. Raskolnikov was in a state of rapture. The rat must have fallen in love with Marianna Storm. His whole body started to wiggle. Dougy had to shout above the rat's song.

"You gonna whack me, Isaac? That's the only way you'll get me out of here."

He rubbed the rat's nose, and Raskolnikov quieted down. Then he turned his back on Isaac and walked away.

"Uncle," Marianna said, "who is that man?"

Part Three

8

The warhorse was coming to town, Michael Storm, who could have stayed with Clarice on Sutton Place South. But New York was Sidel's territory, and J. Michael had to give the impression that he was a man of the United States. The Storm-Sidel Election Committee had booked a suite for him at the Waldorf, Michael's Manhattan address. Michael wanted his own kingdom, like John Fitzgerald Kennedy, who lived at the Waldorf while he was away from the White House. But Michael didn't have a billionaire dad behind him, a family of Boston Irish brahmins. His own mom and dad were kindergarten teachers. He'd saved baseball, settled a wildcat strike, but he was only an ex–student radical who'd swerved a little to the right.

He would have had Sidel killed if he could. Sidel was poisoning his future presidency. But he'd never win without that sheriff from the Lower East Side. He lagged behind his own running mate in all the polls. And the knowledge of it gnawed at him. Seligman was preening Michael, had picked him to address an international association of optometrists, who'd taken over the Waldorf. Michael wouldn't even have to leave the hotel. But he didn't want Isaac dashing around the city with his Glock. He ordered Seligman to put Isaac under house arrest. The mayor was a prisoner in his own mansion.

Isaac didn't rebel. He could live outside the dream of politics for a little while. It was his first vacation in years. But he couldn't stop thinking of Doug Jr., that resurrected Christ. The Maldavanka felt more like a home to him than Gracie Mansion. The Big Guy launched armies in his head. He'd shut down Elizabeth Street, rescue Margaret Tolstoy, find Alyosha. But he couldn't move while Michael was in town.

The baseball czar phoned from the Waldorf. He didn't want to speak to Isaac. He growled until Marianna got on the line.

"You never see me," Michael said. "I'm your dad."

"I'm looking for Alyosha."

"That brat, the muralist?"

"He's missing."

"Sure," Michael said. "He does a lot of damage for a missing boy. He's sabotaging my campaign. He draws Sidel. Why not me?"

"You're not his hero," Marianna said.

"Who's paying him? The FBI, or the Cottonwood Reelection Committee?"

"I'll hang up on you, Father, if you keep talking like that."

"So formal with your own fucking dad? . . . get me Sidel."

Marianna handed the phone to Isaac, who hadn't talked to

J. Michael since the convention. Michael wouldn't even say hello to his running mate.

"That's how you keep my little girl, huh, you prick?"

"What's eating you, J.? Haven't I been docile enough? I sit here like a rat in his manger. Aren't you happy?"

"Have my little girl at the Waldorf in half an hour, or I'll take her from you, I swear to God. No more cookies, Isaac."

Michael hung up and Isaac had to plead with Marianna Storm. "If you don't listen to him, we'll all suffer."

"Uncle Isaac, he tried to murder my mom."

"Shhh," Isaac said. "There could be a hundred different agencies tapping my phone."

"He hired Bernardo Dublin, didn't he? And Mom's so pathetic, she could only fall in love with a man who came to kill her."

"Marianna, please."

"Well, isn't Bernardo her lover and her bodyguard?"

"If you don't go to Michael, I'll lose you. I'm not your guardian. I have no legal claim. And what will I do here? Practically an old man."

"What about Alyosha?"

"I'll put Boyle on the case. The Secret Service will find him."

"Boyle doesn't even know what Alyosha looks like."

"We'll lend him a photograph."

"We don't have any, darling."

"Come on, the kid's on file with the Bronx brigade."

"Why would the police have Alyosha's photograph?"

"Wasn't he a member of the Jokers? Well, the cops photographed the entire gang . . . hurry up."

And Marianna rode down to the Waldorf with her Secret Service man. Raskolnikov kept flashing in front of her eyes, the rat who could cling to a man's neck like a monkey, but the monkey she remembered had such suffering eyes . . .

The Waldorf couldn't impress her, even if it contained an entire block, and was like an ocean liner stranded in some dead sea it had swallowed up. She knew that presidents stayed there, that eccentric millionaires lived in the towers and never had to leave the Waldorf. She ran up the green-carpeted stairs on the Park Avenue side of the hotel, with Joe Montaigne just behind her. There were fresh-cut flowers in tiny urns on tables at the top of the stairs. Marianna didn't even bother to look at the murals on the walls, but she did notice the bored lady pianist who sat on her bench in the cocktail terrace like an angel held in position by invisible strings.

Secret Service men with plugs in their ears seemed to rule the lobby. They winked at Joe Montaigne and whispered into button mikes pinned to their lapels. A riot almost erupted as Marianna was recognized. "The little first lady, the little first lady." Joe Montaigne had to rush her into an elevator car that took her to the towers.

She got out of the car and was greeted by other Secret Service men with plugs in their ears. They escorted Marianna to Michael's suite, while Montaigne waited outside the door.

Tim Seligman sat near the window in a room that was like an enormous terrace. She could have floated out the window and sat on one of the gargoyles of the Chrysler Building. That's how Marianna felt. Tim was with some blonde who must have been Michael's bimbo. She clutched a notebook and had a blank, bewildered look on her face.

"Marianna, meet Gloria, your father's new secretary." Gloria blinked. The absence in her eyes made Marianna remember Raskolnikov more and more.

"Where's the candidate?"

"In bed. He has the blues."

"Then why was I summoned here, Mr. Seligman? Am I his nurse?"

"Hon," Tim said, "you're invaluable to us. The country's crazy about you . . . I was hoping you might cheer him up."

"I'm inhuman, made of ice. Didn't Daddy tell you that?"

"But you're our last resort. If we can't get him out of bed and downstairs to that optometrists' convention, we're up the creek."

"Where is he?" Marianna asked, looking at Gloria of the absent eyes.

Seligman opened a door and Marianna went into Michael's bedroom. Her dad was lying under the covers, in a kingsized bed. He looked like a beetle.

"Baby," Michael whispered. He'd been crying. "I'm lonely. I'll win the election and I'll be the president nobody wants. It's all Sidel, Sidel, Sidel."

"Have you taken your Valium?"

"It's worthless. Like peppermint candy."

"Then what's the solution? Seligman can find you a bed at a nice, cozy clinic, but how will you campaign from there?"

"You could love me a little. That would be a start."

"Tell me you didn't hire Bernardo Dublin to throw Mom out the window."

"I was confused," Michael said. "But I figured Clarice would fall for him."

"That was only a wild guess," Marianna said. "He wasn't hired to fall in love, though I have to admit that he's cute. And I might have fallen for him myself under the same circumstances."

"Stop that. You're my little girl."

"Get out of bed! Right this minute."

"I can't. I'm paralyzed. My feet are frozen."

Marianna pulled the covers off her dad. He was wearing silk pajamas. His feet weren't frozen at all.

"Do you want that bimbo to dress you? Or should I call in the Secret Service?"

"What bimbo? Who's been teaching you such words?"

"Mom," Marianna said. "She likes to talk about your bimbos. It's her favorite topic."

"I couldn't survive without Gloria. She keeps all my records."

"Where? In what part of her anatomy?"

"Stop that. You behave." And Michael began to shout. "Gloria, come here."

The blonde rushed into the bedroom. She had a gorgeous body, Marianna had to admit. But Clarice had much more character, even if she was fascinated with a detective who had murder on his mind.

The blonde shucked off Michael's pajamas, gave him a quick sponge bath, combed his hair, buttoned him into a clean white shirt, selected a dark suit and a paisley tie, and Michael almost looked like a man who could be president.

"It isn't fair," Michael said. "I'm at the Waldorf. Shouldn't I have the Presidential Suite? They said Calder might get mad.

Imagine. Any civilian can rent it out if he's willing to pay the price, but not me."

"Father, what are you complaining about? You'll inherit that suite soon enough. Meanwhile you have all the luxury in the world. It's still the Waldorf."

"I know, I know. But I wanted to sit at FDR's desk. It comes with the suite."

"Who's FDR?" the blonde asked.

Marianna ignored her, but Michael kissed her on the nose.

"J.," she said, "couldn't I come downstairs with you and listen to your speech?"

"And create a scandal? Tim would murder us. You'll wait right here for me."

"But can't I listen, J.? I won't bother anybody. I'll be as quiet as a mouse."

Marianna felt a surge of sympathy for the blonde. "I'll bring her. Gloria can sit with me. We'll say she's with the Secret Service."

And she marched out of the room with Gloria and Michael. Tim started to scream. "Gloria doesn't go near the ballroom."

"Come on. Mr. Seligman, Gloria's my guest."

"With all the reporters racing around? I don't need rumors about a wrecked marriage. Gloria stays here."

Marianna couldn't bear to look at the sadness and sudden animation in Gloria's eyes. Tim whisked her out of the suite, and Michael's party went down a private elevator to the Grand Ballroom. Marianna had never been inside such a place. It had two balconies and a bunch of chandeliers, like an opera house.

The lighting was very soft. Nothing ever blazed at the Waldorf.

She had to climb onto the platform with Tim and her dad. People sat behind long tables that stretched across the ballroom like some telescope that was half alive. The optometrists and their wives were all staring at Marianna. She wouldn't perform for them. Marianna wasn't in the mood. She was still dreaming of Raskolnikov.

Tim introduced her dad, but Marianna wasn't listening. She could only catch clumps of words. "A hero of our time . . . J. Michael Storm."

The optometrists clapped. Her dad did a little dance, smiled at Marianna, grabbed the sides of the podium and delivered a speech that Tim must have designed for him. He blabbed about the significance of optometry to the nation. Marianna felt nauseous. She wanted to scream. She was in the grip of a terrible vertigo while her dad droned on and on. But if she tumbled off the platform, her father's ratings would keep going down.

She survived the speech. Then she disappeared, ducked out on her Secret Service man, got into a cab.

"Maldavanka," she said. "And please hurry."

The driver didn't recognize Marianna Storm. He was quite suspicious. "What Maldavanka? Where is it? Brooklyn? The Bronx?"

"Manhattan," Marianna said.

"There's no such neighborhood. Maldavanka."

"It's near Elizabeth Street."

"That's Chinatown."

"Maybe," Marianna said. "But it's also the Maldavanka."

The driver dropped her off near the stationhouse. Marianna poked through her bag, pulled out the necessary cash, while cops spied on her from the stationhouse steps. She didn't stay very long. She wandered eastward, into the badlands, her imagination stuck on an educated rat.

Buildings began to disappear, whole streets. She walked in a kind of endless rubble. There weren't many walls where Alyosha could have exercised his art. She heard a whistling noise. Three men were behind her, dressed in curious clothes, like soldiers or sailors who were also clowns. They had long hats and winter coats in the summer heat. They had combat boots with broken heels, colored handkerchiefs wrapped around their raw, red throats.

They flirted with Marianna. "Hiya, sweetie pie."

But she wouldn't flirt back. They crept close to her, bottles of wine hanging out of their big pockets.

"Hold it, sis. We'll give you a guided tour."

They reached out to touch her with their filthy hands. She hissed at them. But they surrounded Marianna, and she couldn't run.

"We wanna play, that's all. Couldn't you do the hootchy-kootchy and take off some of your clothes?"

They took her bag away, knocked her to the ground, removed their hats, and stood above her with their swollen faces.

And then time seemed to stop. They stood motionless, mesmerized by a metallic screech that almost burst Marianna's ears. A pair of claws with eyes and razorlike teeth swooped down upon them in an instant, like a little monster that had learned to fly without wings. It was Raskolnikov.

The rat bit their faces as he swerved through the air. The three men howled and started to run. They stopped in their tracks, got down on their knees. "Maestro," they said, "maestro, we didn't mean to antagonize your animal. Look at her clothes. How could we figure that Raskolnikov had a rich friend?"

That's when she discovered the outlaw in the orange pants, with Raskolnikov on his shoulder.

"Shut up," he said to the three men, "and get out of my sight."

They wanted to kiss the outlaw's hand, but Raskolnikov squealed at them, and they ran.

The outlaw helped Marianna off the ground. "We were never introduced," he said. "I'm Douglas Knight Jr. I'm not supposed to be alive."

"Who were those men?"

"Weaklings . . . winos."

"Do they work for you?"

"No. I ought to cancel their tickets. But I can't kill everybody."

"Why is this place called the Maldavanka? There's no Maldavanka in Manhattan. That's what a cabdriver told me."

"Well, cabdrivers could be wrong . . . it's a name out of a book. Like Camelot. But there was a Maldavanka once. On the Black Sea. I'm not sure that Maldavanka still exists."

"It moved to Manhattan?"

"Something like that."

"Did you see my fiancé? Angel Carpenteros. Calls himself Alyosha. He draws pictures of Uncle Isaac on the walls."

The outlaw laughed. "With the eyes of Che Guevara? No, I haven't seen him. Come on. Let's eat."

They entered a little diner that sat among the ruins. The outlaw didn't have to order a meal. Rice and beans arrived, with bits of ham, toasted bread, a salad, and a bottle of dark beer.

"Drink with me," the outlaw said, pouring from his bottle. "It's the badlands. We can break the law."

Marianna drank the beer. She burped once, excused herself. "Why aren't you supposed to be alive?"

"Because I made a fuss. I wanted to change things. I had to hurt some people. The whole goddamn government came down on my head. It's a long story. I worked for the President once."

"President Cottonwood cares about the Maldavanka?"

"Nah. He was just scoring points. But I care. So they had to pretend . . ."

"Pretend?"

"Pretend to kill me. I promised to leave the badlands. I was given a fat bank account, another name. Melvin or Marvin. I can't remember. But I couldn't leave. And now they've stopped pretending."

"Then you should come and live with us. At Gracie Mansion. Uncle Isaac will take you in."

"Marianna," the outlaw said, "my home is here."

And she couldn't argue with him. Men and women came up to the outlaw, dropped crumpled dollar bills in his lap. "El Señor," they said. They saluted Marianna, called her "La Señora."

"El Señor," Marianna repeated. "What does all that money mean?"

"Ah, they think I'm their savior. So they feed me dollar bills. To help the poor. I'm a walking collection box."

"But why are the dollars all crumpled up?"

"To beat the Devil . . . the Devil doesn't like wrinkled money. Gives him heartburn."

"Can I visit you again?"

"Of course. Next time you won't have any problems. They've seen you with me. La Señora."

Raskolnikov hopped off the outlaw's shoulder, stood on his hind legs. He was begging for beer. The outlaw fed him from the bottle, like a baby. Raskolnikov lapped the beer and looked into Marianna's eyes.

"Can I touch him?" she asked.

"Sure. He likes to be stroked. But not by strangers."

She rubbed the rat's bald head. Raskolnikov crooned in his tinny voice and closed his eyes. Then he jumped under the table, ran between Marianna's ankles.

"Quiet," the outlaw said, and Raskolnikov wrapped his tail around a table leg, hanging upside down like a bat. "You got him excited. He isn't usually like that."

She kissed the outlaw on the cheek, said good-bye to Raskolnikov, and one of the men from the diner drove her up to Gracie Mansion. The Secret Service was furious with Marianna. "We were worried," said Joe Montaigne. "We thought it was another kidnapping. You should never jump off our screen."

"You don't have a screen, Joe," she said and walked out onto the porch, sat in a rocking chair next to Isaac, who was still under house arrest, married to his own mansion while J. Michael was in town.

"Sinbad," Isaac said, staring out into the waters of Hell's Gate. He didn't even know Marianna was alive. "Sinbad." He was talking to the sea. Marianna said nothing. She wouldn't contradict her own personal sailor.

9

Sinbad didn't want Dougy to die and die and die again. He couldn't think about election campaigns. If Margaret wasted young Doug, he'd have to get even. But how could Sinbad waste the woman he loved? He'd have to short-circuit her career as a huntress, shove her beyond Bull Latham and the FBI. She could play Scheherazade for the Prez, tell him stories about herself and Isaac. He'd learn to live with that. But he'd have to grab that ghost, Ferdinand Antonescu, who'd outlasted Hitler, Stalin, Khrushchev, and the Cold War, should have gone to Hell years ago but was miraculously alive. Isaac's networks had froze. He was a mayor, out of touch with all the little intelligence teams that had flourished around him when he was the Commish. He had to rely on his Secret Service man, hope Boyle understood that his career depended on Isaac.

He rose out of his stupor, dug the Glock deep into his pants, and summoned Martin Boyle. "Boyle, I need you to help me find a war criminal. Ferdinand Antonescu. He's tucked away somewhere in Virginia. The Bureau is holding him on ice. That's how the Bull makes Margaret dance. He and the Prez have her on a string. Will you comb all the sanitariums near Alexandria for Uncle Ferdinand's address?"

"No problem. I met Antonescu. He's a cold fish."

"The Butcher of Bucharest? You met him? How? Where?"

"At the Riverrun Estates. It's a posh nursing home. Millionaires, senile movie stars, and dinosaur generals. I was Margaret's chauffeur. The Prez would ask me to drive her to Riverrun. As a personal favor."

"Grand," Isaac said. "Then repeat the favor. For old Isaac. Drive me there. I wanna grab that butcher, that son of a bitch. Bring him to Gracie."

"It's a hornet's nest, sir. Riverrun's as tight as Fort Knox. There's too much history packed into that place. For a lot of people, sir, it's the last address they'll ever have."

"Well, we'll have to make an exception, Boyle. Antonescu's mine."

"Sir . . ."

"Boyle, who'll win in November?"

"The Democrats, Mr. President."

"Is your future with Cottonwood or Isaac Sidel?"

"Sidel, sir."

"Then you'll have to be my Virgil."

"I don't get it."

"My guide, Boyle. Virgil took a poet named Dante Alighieri through Hell."

"Hell's a picnic, sir, some kind of big joke, compared to

Riverrun. It's rotten with secret agents . . . probably lose my job."

They got onto the Metroliner, both of them wearing dark glasses. They looked like a pair of contract killers. They avoided the club car, shunned other passengers, ate sandwiches in their seats. Isaac didn't want the stigmata of his own candidacy to follow him into Cottonwood's town. He had to remain anonymous in and around D.C. They arrived at Union Station in their dark glasses, neither of them carrying a businessman's case. They rode out to Alexandria in a taxicab. Isaac removed his dark glasses.

"Sinbad," the driver said, "I'm real glad to meet ya."

Isaac groaned.

"You're the best thing that's happened to this country. I voted Republican all my life. But I'm gonna switch. The President aint no damn good. He abandoned us. Doesn't even know the price of milk."

The driver wouldn't permit Isaac to pay the fare. "Call it a contribution . . . from a born-again Democrat."

Isaac entered Riverrun, which had its own park along the Potomac. It was a glorious estate, with an English garden. How could he convince Uncle Ferdinand to leave this fucking little paradise?

The doctors and nurses seemed to know about his arrival. Boyle waited in the lobby, and Isaac went upstairs to Ferdinand's room. The old man wasn't in a wheelchair. He wore a purple handkerchief in his breast pocket, stood near the door, flowering at eighty-five. The boldness of that handkerchief disarmed Isaac, seemed to announce that Ferdinand was still a sexual creature. Isaac was crazed with jealousy. The criminal had taken Margaret into his bed almost fifty years ago. He handed Isaac a cup of tea and a piece of chocolate cake.

Isaac was ravenous. He finished the cake before he said hello.

"Ferdinand, you don't have a choice. You're coming with me."

"I admire your directness, Monsieur. I wish we'd had the likes of you in Transnistra. We might have won the war."

Isaac wanted to strangle him. Ferdinand had been viceroy of the Nazis' puppet kingdom on the Black Sea. He'd rescued his own tailor and a couple of Jewish aristocrats, but murdered gypsies and orphans, lived on their flesh, like a fucking cannibal. Margaret had eaten the same orphans, or she would have starved. Isaac could forgive a twelve-year-old girl, but not Antonescu.

"You're a pimp," he said.

Antonescu smiled. "Monsieur, I've been called much worse than that."

"Cut the crap. You don't have to be gallant. This isn't Paris, and I'm nobody's *monsieur*. I'm—"

"Sinbad the Sailor. I keep up with the news, Monsieur."

"Margaret slaves for the FBI, works on her back, and you have your run of this little mansion."

"You're a sentimentalist, Monsieur. Margaret loves to work on her back."

"And who trained her?"

"She wasn't such an unwilling pupil."

"Shut the fuck up. You're coming with me."

The Butcher of Bucharest smiled again. "How could I resist you, Monsieur Sidel? You're the younger man. But I have my own grievance. Margaret mentions her other lovers, but she never mentions Sinbad the Sailor. You're her big secret."

"Then who told you about us, Uncle Ferdinand?"

"The Bureau's like a bunch of old wives. Can't stop chatting about the miraculous love affair . . . I'm the wounded party. And I'm locked away in this house."

"Then come with Sinbad. And Margaret won't have to be the Bureau's heavy hitter."

"Why should I trade mansions, Monsieur? I'd have to look at you. And I might want to crush your skull. It doesn't take much to bring out my murderous side . . . no, I think I'll stay at Riverrun."

"Wrong," Isaac said. He grabbed Antonescu's sleeve. The old man didn't resist. He walked downstairs with Isaac. Martin Boyle was gone. But other Secret Service men surrounded Pamela Box, who sat in a plush chair with elephants carved into the armrests. She let Isaac have a peek at her long, muscular legs. Pam must have played badminton with the Prez on the White House lawn. Her husband was an alcoholic professor-poet who scribbled speeches for Calder Cottonwood. He taught at Georgetown from time to time, had his own attic room at the White House. Professor Jonathan Box. And when Pamela pranced around naked with the Prez, the Secret Service fed gin to Jonathan, shoved him into a drunken stupor. Calder's wife had died during his second year in office. She'd been sick when she arrived at the White House, and the Secret Service never had any logistical problems with the First Lady. Pamela ruled Pennsylvania Avenue, and she was also the queen of Riverrun, with her blond hair and blue eyelashes, and her corps of Secret Service men.

"Where's Boyle?" Isaac asked.

"Don't worry. You'll get him back. But he's a bad boy, Sidel. He shouldn't have brought you here . . . hello, Ferdinand. Have you been sleepwalking with the mayor?"

"No, Madame. He was planning to steal me. I told him it was foolish."

"But you might have yelled."

"My lungs are already paper, Madame. And I had a suspicion that you'd be at the bottom of the stairs."

"We're all proud of you, Ferdinand. Go back to your room. I have things to discuss with Sidel."

"You shouldn't treat me like a child, Madame. I had my own secret service in Odessa."

"I know. With Gestapo armbands."

Antonescu turned around and walked upstairs.

Pamela lit a cigarillo. There wasn't much patience in her eyes.

"Calder doesn't like your tricks. Don't come here again."

"Then he shouldn't have used my town as a laboratory."

"Your town? He's President of the United States."

"That doesn't give him the right to train cops as extermination teams."

"He isn't the Butcher of Bucharest. He cleaned up an area that was crawling with criminals and helped create a model precinct."

"Then why is everybody so eager to kill Dougy Knight?"

"He was a wild card. The President gave him his chance. He shouldn't have returned to those ruins. And he's officially dead, isn't he, Sidel?"

"So Margaret hunts down an invisible man."

"Do you have a better idea? Would you like NBC to interview him? . . . he's your baby, Sidel. Get him off the street, or we'll have to give him to Mrs. Tolstoy."

"Mrs. Tolstoy," Isaac muttered. "You mean Madame Antonescu, Ferdinand's bride."

Pamela curled one of her fingers. It was a signal to her Secret Service men. They vanished, left Pamela alone with Isaac in the lobby of Riverrun. She blinked like Cleopatra with blue eyelashes.

"Sidel, pat me down, see if I'm wearing a wire . . . don't be afraid."

She rose from her chair, clasped Isaac's hands, put them on her body. He could have been exploring a map. There was no electricity in her flesh. She was Calder's beautiful, cunning mistress and chief of staff.

He pulled his hands out of Pamela's. "You can wear all the wires you want, Mrs. Box."

She slapped Isaac. His teeth hurt. He sucked on the salt that mingled with his blood. She had no power over him. He hated her blue eyelashes.

"Sidel, we can have an election or total war. You have a wife in the Florida Keys, or did you forget the Countess Kathleen?"

"I thought she moved to Miami."

"She's into Republican politics. We could bribe her, Sidel, script a couple of interviews, offer them to the *Miami Herald*. Voters might not be too happy about a possible vice-president with a wife in the closet."

"You can't bribe Kathleen. She's richer than the Prez. And

if you want to get down and dirty, Mrs. Box, I could script a couple of interviews about Calder's little harems."

"He's a widower," Pam said. "He's entitled to a harem."

"In the White House, Mrs. Box? Tell that to Alabama and Tennessee."

"We have a file on you, sonny, that could fill a room."

"Fuck your file," Isaac said. He grabbed Pamela, kissed her on the mouth with all the poison he could produce. She trembled in his arms. Her vulnerability troubled Isaac. He preferred Pam as a dragon lady or a queen bee. He ran out of Riverrun, found Martin Boyle in the back of a Secret Service sedan.

"Judas," Isaac said. "You told them I was coming to Riverrun. Pamela's your real boss."

"We're a fraternity, Mr. President, one tribe, but I didn't have to tell. Pam's clairvoyant. She can anticipate all your moves."

"All my moves, huh? The White House witch. Who wired Gracie Mansion for the Prez? Joe Montaigne or you?"

"Sir, it was wired long before we moved in. Bull Latham has everybody's handle."

"Grand," Isaac said, and he growled at the driver. "Will you take me and this thug out of Virginia? We have a train to catch."

He couldn't escape Alyosha's murals. The kid drew him with a full black beard and a blacker beret. The drawings appeared on television screens: Isaac in the garb of a revolutionary. Republicans clapped their hands. The guy they feared the most had turned into Che Guevara. Isaac should have fallen in the polls. But he was identified with the hurlyburly of Manhattan, where Guevara was one more lost soul who could rise out of the grave and travel from wall to wall.

Tim Seligman began offering rewards, but no one could capture the muralist. Isaac took to the sky again with Marianna Storm. He returned without a clue. And then the guard telephoned him from the mansion's gate. "We have a couple of characters, sir. A runt and some clown with a blanket."

"I'm in the middle of a conference," Isaac said, munching on Marianna's cookies. "Tell 'em to scram."

"The clown insists that he has a friend who knows you."

"What friend?"

"Somebody called Raskolnikov."

"Jesus," Isaac shouted. "Will ya let 'em in?"

And young Doug entered the mansion looking like Christ in a blanket. Angel Carpenteros was with him. He had specks of blood on his face. Dougy removed the blanket, revealed his orange pants and a soulful Russian rat curled around his neck. Marianna came down from her bedroom, smiled at the outlaw, and rushed over to Alyosha.

"What happened to your face?"

"The Jokers found me. This hombre saved my life," he said, pointing to young Doug.

"I had to get him out of there."

"Grand," Isaac said. "This isn't the Maldavanka, where you can play Benya Krik. Bull Latham will know that you surfaced. You'll have to accept the sanctuary of a mayor's house."

"Not a chance. It's much too clean for Raskolnikov."

"Then we'll get it dirty. We'll build him a nest."

The rat looked at Marianna Storm, leapt off Dougy's

shoulder, spun around in midair, and landed on a couch, wailing his own lamentable love song. The maid heard Raskolnikov's metallic sound, ran into the living room, saw Raskolnikov, and started to scream.

"Your Honor, there aren't any rodents in my contract."

"Miranda, he's an intellectual. And he has feelings . . . like a human being."

"I don't care. A rat's a rat."

And she stormed out of the living room, while Raskolnikov did another somersault and reached the chandelier, without taking his eyes off Marianna.

Isaac was perplexed. He turned to Alyosha. His hands started to tremble.

"You wanna ruin us, kid? First you escape from Peekskill, and I'm responsible for you. And then you exercise your art at my expense. You draw me as Che Guevara."

"You are the Che," Alyosha said. "You're a revolutionary."

"Shhh," Isaac said. "What if the Grand Old Party hears that? I'm on the Democratic ticket. The Republicans will slaughter me."

"You're a dreamer. Your head's in the clouds. Like the Che."

"But I didn't die in Bolivia," Isaac said. "I wanna help New York. It's not the same thing."

Marianna grabbed Alyosha's hand, while Raskolnikov dug deeper into the glass twigs of the chandelier.

"Darling," she said to Isaac, "you'll have to let him live here with us."

"And if Children's Court finds out? I'll be arrested."

"Who will arrest you? You're practically president."

"Did you forget about your dad?"

"He's just a temporary toothache," Marianna said. "He'll go away."

She smiled at young Doug, blew a kiss to the rat inside the chandelier, and went onto the porch with Alyosha.

Raskolnikov lost his interest in Isaac's house. He stopped exploring, and jumped back onto Dougy's shoulder.

"How can I protect you?" Isaac said. "You're on the President's irrevocable shitlist."

"I'd consider that a compliment."

"Your parents are in exile. They'll never survive the Arizona sun."

"Wrong," Dougy said. "Mom and Dad talked of retiring to Scottsdale for years. They collected brochures."

"Brochures?" Isaac said. "It's like collecting stamps."

"I would have gone to Scottsdale too. I would have joined them."

"With Daniella Grossvogel?"

"Daniella's not your business, Mr. Mayor."

"Does she know you're still alive?"

"I couldn't tell her. She'd have come looking for me. She'd have gotten right in the middle of the crossfire."

"Grand," Isaac said. "She'll have to mourn you twice . . . and what if Captain Bart told her?"

"I doubt it. What would he say? 'Daniella, your own little Doug walked out of the grave and I'll have to kill him.' Bart's too much of a coward. He'll play silent with his daughter. He always does."

"And you? You run back into the badlands with your bodyguard. How long will you and Raskolnikov last?"

"Long enough."

"Even if you escape Margaret Tolstoy, Captain Bart and the Bull will send other hunters after you."

"It's my territory now. They're the strangers. I'll do a little salsa in the streets, dance around the bullets . . ."

"Like a matador, huh?"

"The Prez had Margaret and me clean up the place. We knocked off the bad guys, and then Captain Bart moved in, grabbed whatever he could, until I chased him out with all his men. Was I supposed to go on a permanent holiday, sit in the sun, while Bart was plundering people? I didn't have a choice."

"But I could go after Bart."

Dougy laughed to himself. "It would be like kissing a mirage. He's connected."

"So am I."

"Excuse me, sir, but all you are is a candidate pissing in the wind."

"Not after November."

"November? That's light years away. I can't think past tomorrow."

He rubbed Raskolnikov's back, said good-bye, and walked out of Gracie Mansion. And Isaac was left all alone, like Sinbad stranded in some ocean he couldn't even recall.

IO

He couldn't stop thinking of Daniella. Doug was her Odessa man, her Benya Krik. He could have gone down to Washington Square Village and knocked on her door . . . he didn't have to knock. Doug had her key. But the doorman knew his face, and Doug was supposed to be dead. She'd tutored him at the precinct. He was studying for the sergeant's test, like all the idiots of Elizabeth Street. The other cops made fun of her, called Daniella a beast. But Dougy didn't mind the boil on her back. She was like a shooting star with a radiance sitting on her shoulder. And when she talked of that gangster in the orange pants, he'd watch her lips move, and he fell in love with the daughter of a captain he despised. He had battles in the locker room. No one was allowed to call Daniella a beast . . .

He didn't stop at Washington Square Village. He went directly to the Maldavanka, with Raskolnikov tucked under his blanket. He got out of the cab, gave the blanket to a grandma sitting on a sofa at the corner of Henry and Clinton, and started to travel south. Sidel had been right. Elizabeth Street must have known that he'd left the badlands, because Captain Bart was waiting for him near the Rutgers housing project, with five or six of his boys. He wasn't worried. He had Raskolnikov and a Glock in his pants. All he had to do was touch the rat's tail, and Raskolnikov would have clawed Barton's eyes out.

It was Bart who was nervous.

"You keep the rat on your shoulder, hear?"

"Anything," Doug said, "anything for my future father-in-law."

"Stop that," the captain said. "My Daniella aint marrying a dead man . . . we have you six to one. Will ya go to Arizona, where you belong? We're not FBI. We're simple cops. We don't shoot one of our own."

Dougy didn't like Barton's song. The captain was stroking him, and then Doug realized what the song was about. Barton began to smile.

"Will ya finish him, for God's sake?" Barton said to someone behind Doug, and Dougy didn't have to turn. It was Margaret Tolstoy. He could smell Margaret's perfume. She appeared in the corner of his eye. She was much more clever than Bart. She had a Glock in one hand and a broom in the other. She meant to slap Raskolnikov out of the air.

"Hello, Dougy," she said.

The captain's eyes were bulging. "Stop palavering, woman. Kill him."

"Not today."

"What's wrong with today? You were hired to kill him, Mrs. Tolstoy. Didn't we plan it like that?"

"You planned it, Bart. I just nodded my head."

"I work for the White House. Don't you?"

"Some of the time."

"And what if I talked to the Bull? You'll lose your paycheck and your pension . . . and that ancient husband of yours in Alexandria."

"You ought to be more respectful of Ferdinand. He ran a whole country."

"I can't believe it," Barton said. "The Bull lends us his ace, and she treats us like a bunch of niggers . . . boys, we'll have to do the both of them."

"I'm protected," Margaret said. "I have the broom. Can you imagine what Raskolnikov will do to your face before you pull your trigger . . . and then I'll shoot off your kneecaps."

"She's a psychopath. I never trusted her. She undresses for the President. That's how he gets it off."

"Shall I remind Calder of what you said about him? He'll love it, Bart. He'll pull you right out of the picture."

"You won't remind him of anything . . . boys?"

And that's when Barton heard Raskolnikov's metallic scream. He lost his bite and his ambition. He had no more battle plans. He withdrew without a word, his six cops paddling behind him.

Margaret put down the broom, and Raskolnikov jumped on her shoulder. She didn't flinch. Doug watched her stroke the rat's belly.

"Should I thank you, Margaret?"

"No. I'll have to come back. But without Bart. I owe you that bit of courtesy . . . take care of yourself."

"I saw Sinbad. He looks sad without you."

"He's always sad . . . good-bye, Dougy. And get the hell out of here. People can spot you a mile away in your orange pants."

She kissed him on the mouth, and Raskolnikov traded shoulders, returned to Doug.

She was the best partner Dougy ever had. The two of them could have tamed the whole Wild West. She'd tell him stories about the Maldavanka during World War II, when there were no Benya Kriks around, and any Jewish gangster in orange pants would have been lucky to be alive. "The Maldavanka was piss-poor. It was overrun with rats, and they didn't have Raskolnikov's charm. They'd chew the fingers off a boy in a baby carriage . . . you should know better, kid. I love books. I'm a reader. But literature's a dangerous thing."

He liked it when she called him "kid." But she couldn't destroy Benya, not even with all her ramblings. Heck, you had to have a hero. Benya fed the poor with fat cows he stole from the rich. There were no cows near Elizabeth Street. And Dougy had depleted his small fortune riding up to Gracie Mansion and riding down. He had a few crumpled dollar bills in his pocket. He'd have to rip off a couple of policemen, but Bart's own little boys kept out of sight, unless they arrived with the captain himself in regular war parties.

Doug could fall asleep in any abandoned building. Raskolnikov would wake him. The rat was like a master sergeant. Doug had to smile. He noticed a drawing of Sidel in a beard and beret on a Cherry Street wall. But he couldn't linger, couldn't stop to admire the authenticity of Alyosha's art. That wall was a magnet for the Latin Jokers. He'd snatched Alyosha away from the gang. They were frightened of Raskolnikov, had to protect their faces from a rat who could fly in the air. He might have shot a Joker in the foot if he had to. But he wouldn't have really glocked them. They were kids. They couldn't even grow a proper mustache.

He smoked his last cigarette, let Raskolnikov have a puff. The rat was crazy about tobacco, loved to nibble on it. Raskolnikov lived on cigarettes and ice cream and the dark earth of the Maldavanka. The earth had minerals that brightened the color of Raskolnikov's coat. But how long would the orange in Dougy's pants last? There were no dry cleaners in the badlands. He had to depend on the kindness of certain grandmas, who would wash and iron Dougy's pants in the basement of some hovel near the East River. He had his parishioners. He was almost like a priest . . . or a constable. He had to give up his badge, so *something* could be pinned on the corpse that was picked to play Doug. But he was getting a little tired. He wasn't a strategist like Benya Krik. He didn't have a master plan. And how could he revive *this* Maldavanka, a world of abandoned buildings and housing projects that had a relentless silhouette, without the least decoration, the least human line?

He wasn't surprised when he saw them. Raskolnikov had already rattled his tail and hissed. Ten Jokers with long knives, their faces covered with catchers' masks. They were the ones with a strategy, not Doug. They'd adapted to Raskolnikov in under a day. He felt like smiling, because the Jokers had a medieval look, like knights in the wilderness. He could have outrun their knives, or let Raskolnikov attack their groins. But he was weary of war. He wouldn't attack children, and how could he flee his own territory? He was El Señor, who had the status of a king with crumpled bills in his pockets.

The Jokers surrounded him.

"Homey," they said, "you should have given us our puta. We have no quarrel with you. You're like a holy man in this 'hood. But Angel Carpenteros is on our death list."

"Fine. But I wouldn't have let you kill him."

"Then take out your Glock, man, and duel with us a little."

"I only duel with enemies," Doug said. And he began to wonder. Was it Captain Bart who'd supplied them with the catchers' masks? Were they part of the captain's team? It didn't matter. He still wouldn't attack them. He had to clutch Raskolnikov, prevent him from leaping on the Jokers. But he could feel Raskolnikov's heart beat, feel the bristling skin of a warrior rat.

"Niños," he said, "are you with the police or the FBI?"

"Both," they said.

He still wouldn't fight. He remembered Daniella's smile. But there wasn't much else in the world that he'd miss. Only Raskolnikov. And his poor mom and dad. He plucked Raskolnikov off his shoulder, pushed him deep under a rock, because he knew that these kids were capable of burning a rat alive, and bringing his carcass back to Bull Latham.

"Raski," he said, "listen to me. Don't you come out from that rock."

And then he stood up straight in his orange pants, bowed to the Latin Jokers.

"Niños," he said, "come on and play."

But he didn't go for his Glock.

Part Four

II

It was like a separate village with its own nickname, the Infirmary, and a Marine who guarded its stairs. No one could enter without revealing his or her ID. Margaret wore a special badge that Calder himself had given her. She was part of the Infirmary's hectic, hidden elite. It was supposed to have been a little hospital during the Civil War, a place where colonels and generals of the Union might convalesce. And Margaret wondered if these colonels and generals still haunted the attic on Pennsylvania Avenue.

Half the attic was like a hotel with the President's houseguests. Pam's own husband lived here. The other half was a haven for the President's harebrained cabals. Calder loved intrigue, couldn't exist without it. And Margaret never questioned the rough-and-tumble women and men who seemed to loiter in the halls among the more intellectual types, a band of architects put in the attic to build phantom housing projects for the Prez. There were models of these phantom projects all over the place. Margaret kept bumping into papier mâché towers. One tower started to move. Margaret smiled at the sudden metamorphosis. It was Pam's drunken spouse, Dr. Jonathan Box, camouflaged as a building. He wore a Browning Barracuda in his pants, like other cowboys in the attic. He'd threatened to shoot a couple of chandeliers with his 9 mm cannon, but Margaret wasn't even sure he knew how to fire a gun. He was the Republican Party's chief theoretician. Calder cuckolded him as often as he could, but the Prez had stopped sleeping with Pam.

"I'll bite your titties," the professor told Margaret. "I'm crazy about you, kid."

"Jon, cut it out."

"Calder can't have everything . . . and don't rile me, Margaret. Remember, I have a gun."

She tapped him gently, and the tower that he was playing started to tumble. Margaret grabbed him in time, propped Jonathan against a wall.

"You be good," she said.

"Margaret, I'll try."

The Prez had created a madhouse under his own roof, where he could pretend to be powerless, fulfill the fantasies of a boy with mischief on his mind. He'd also built an outsized nursery with enormous cribs and hobbyhorses. Before Jonathan had moved into the attic, the Prez would sneak Pamela up there, dress her in a little gown, have her climb into one of the cribs. But the nursery was idle now. And Margaret liked to sit and contemplate in a corner of the room. It reminded her of her childhood, when she had a hobbyhorse she could ride endlessly and dream. And perhaps the attic was an instrument of Calder's desire to dream away his presidency.

Margaret entered the room, saw the curl of cigarette smoke. She wasn't alone. Pamela stood between the cribs.

"Has Jon been a nuisance?"

"It's nothing, Pam."

They tried to be civil for the President's sake. Pam was the wounded one. Margaret had replaced her in the President's own curious affections. But all Margaret cared about was that ragamuffin, Sidel. Pam almost felt sorry for Mrs. Tolstoy.

"He's been asking for you," Pam said. "He's nervous."

"Who?"

"The Powerhouse."

The two rivals laughed. Cottonwood, that ladies' man, hadn't had an erection in months. Margaret and Pamela were giggling like schoolgirls. But they stopped when the Powerhouse appeared. He must have swiped the Barracuda from Professor Jon. He had grease around his eyes, nightfighter paint that the Marine at the door had lent him. He preferred the attic to the Oval Office. He loved to romp around, start war games with whatever Marines were available. He removed a solid silver flask from his pocket, sucked on it, then wiped his mouth. His blue eyes narrowed, pinkened like a rat's.

"Pam," he said, "nobody invited you into my meditation room. Get the hell out of here."

He tossed the flask at her. It struck the wall, and whiskey splashed over their heads.

Pam cooed at him. "Calder, you ought to take a nap."

"Shut up. I have business with Margaret."

"But you're tired. Did you forget? You're having dinner

tonight with all the arts and humanities people. You have to freshen up."

"Fuck the arts and humanities people. Scram, before I lock you in one of the cribs."

"I wouldn't mind. You've always been my jailor, Mr. President."

He shoved her out of the room, locked the door, and approached Margaret with the gun in his hand. She didn't budge. She was like some kind of spectator in Calder's attic. The blue had come back into his eyes. He dug the Barracuda into her cheek.

"If you point a gun at a girl, Mr. President, you'd better fire it or get fucked."

"You can't talk to me like that."

"Why not? What will you do? Get rid of me like you got rid of young Doug? Bury my brains in the Rose Garden?"

"That hooligan cop was your responsibility, and you flubbed it. He could have wrecked my whole campaign."

"Then you're off to a sorry start. You can't fix those badlands, Calder. Not even Isaac can."

"But I can fix you and that little mayor of yours."

Margaret walloped him. He crashed into a crib. The Barracuda fell out of his hand.

"You hit me. You struck the President."

"Aw," Margaret said, "come to Mama." She had to defuse him, smother his violent dreams. She held out her arms, and he stumbled toward her. Margaret ran her fingers along the ridges of his war paint. She didn't feel like cuddling him in a mammoth crib, taking off her clothes, like some Salome.

"Isaac," he said, "it's always Isaac. You were with genuine

warriors, Nazi captains and colonels, and that degenerate, Antonescu. But at least he was an adult. How could you have fallen in love with a stinking schoolboy on the Lower East Side? . . . ah, I already know. Love has its own lightning. But it's a lot of crap."

"Then what are you complaining about?"

"Can't I complain? A schoolboy. He hadn't even sentenced anyone to death."

"Maybe that's what I liked about him. He had Odessa in his brown eyes. Isaac could make a girl remember the sea."

"And what about Calder Cottonwood?"

"He's stuck inside the bars of a crib."

Margaret saw that delicious jolt of pain cross in front of his eyes. He had his fix for the afternoon. He wouldn't rush around with a gun, bother Pamela Box. His forehead crinkled under the war paint.

"Don't be stingy," he said. "I'll kill you if you leave out a single detail. You're a little girl in ragged clothes. It's your first day in class. You come through the door, the starving princess who danced across an ocean. Tell me. Tell me. What do you see?"

She had him now. Calder was hooked. He'd be in rapture soon as Scheherazade started to sing.

12

Nothing was reported. There was no news about a missing man in the Maldavanka. But Isaac dreamt of Dougy, saw the blood. He woke with a shiver on his rosewood bed, a priceless antique handed down from mayor to mayor. There was a knock on his door. He climbed out of the blankets in his blue pajamas. He fumbled with the combination lock, let his Secret Service man into the room.

"Dougy's dead, isn't he, Boyle?"

"I think so, Mr. President."

"Is it a fucking hypothesis?"

"No, sir. It's a fact."

"Did Captain Bart knock him off?"

"Indirectly, sir."

"Boyle, it's too early in the morning for riddles. Can't you see? I'm shaking all over. What happened?"

"I don't have all the details, sir. But I suspect Bull paid Captain Bart to hire the assassination team."

"Was Margaret with that team?"

"Well, sir . . . she was and she wasn't."

"Will you stop talking Chinese?"

"She made contact with Doug . . . but that was before the second team arrived."

"There were two fucking teams? Have the major leagues come to the badlands? . . . Boyle, I'm going back to bed."

"Sir, it's less complicated than you think. Captain Bart arrived with his goon squad. But Margaret made him abort. She wouldn't allow Bart to hammer Doug."

"She saved his hide?"

"Exactly, sir . . . and then the second team showed up with rather strange gear . . . catchers' masks."

"Bart wanted to neutralize Raskolnikov, didn't he?"

"Sir, he lent the masks to the Latin Jokers and gave them pocket money."

"The Jokers did Dougy?"

"That's the scenario, sir. And Bart buried him, God knows where. I doubt that we'll ever find Doug."

"And you got that information from your fucking fishwives at the Secret Service."

"No, sir. Joe Montaigne has a cousin who's pretty close to some temp at Elizabeth Street. She caught the captain celebrating with his men."

"And where's Raskolnikov, where's Dougy's rat?"

"The rat wasn't discussed, according to that clerk."

"Boyle," Isaac said, "I'm mayor, Manhattan's Big Man, and your lousy little network is better than mine."

Isaac got into his clothes and fled Gracie Mansion with Boyle right behind him. They were like a couple of ghosts.

Isaac couldn't walk a step in Washington Square Village without scribbling his autograph. A woman dropped her grocery bags and kissed Isaac. "I'll die," she said. "Isaac, you're so handsome."

With all his gloom, the Big Guy couldn't resist such spontaneous warmth. He danced with the woman, did a little fox-trot he remembered from his days at Seward Park High, when he was a thug with sideburns, a delinquent who would move on to marry the Countess Kathleen. It was Kathleen's Irish connections at the NYPD that had saved Isaac Sidel. The Irish took him in because of his bride, and he rose relentlessly, from undercover cop to Commish. He would have gotten nowhere without his Irish rabbis.

He went upstairs to Daniella Grossvogel. She wore a red robe that seemed to highlight her lovely face. She didn't need lipstick. Isaac felt like proposing to her. He made a fist to keep from crying.

"Would you like some coffee, Mr. Mayor?"

"Daniella, I can't lie to you. Dougy's dead."

"Sit down, please. Should I call a doctor? You look feverish."

"That other death, it was a fake. The FBI set it up. Dougy was supposed to disappear. But he stayed in the badlands."

She collapsed onto her couch, pale now in her red robe. "How can I believe you? I would have known . . . I went to his funeral, Mr. Mayor."

"Daniella, did they ever open the box?"

"But there were horrible wounds. His father . . ."

"Captain Knight never touched his son. He's a cop, the best. The Bureau moved him to Arizona."

"But Dougy would have . . ."

"How could he visit you? He was running from the FBI and your dad."

"I would have heard him . . . in my heart."

"You did hear him, Daniella. Every time you lectured about Benya Krik . . . he couldn't leave that rotten community. He wanted his own Maldavanka. He wanted you."

"But I could have . . ."

"He was afraid something would happen, that you'd go down there, get hurt."

Isaac sat with her on the couch. She was the one who held Isaac in her arms, rocked the mayor, like she was reading a lullaby to him. "Doug never wanted to be a sergeant, not really. But he enjoyed the lessons. He was my ablest pupil. He couldn't live without words. He read and read and read . . ."

Isaac was blubbering now. "Daniella, I'm so sorry. Maybe I could have . . ."

"He was doomed. I shouldn't have introduced him to Benya Krik. He was an outcast, couldn't relate to cops."

"No, Daniella. He was the cop. And your father's men were the chiselers."

He stopped blubbering. Daniella had revived him. They hugged each other like orphans might have hugged. But Isaac was already dreaming murder.

He collected Boyle outside Daniella's building and marched across SoHo to the Maldavanka. He avoided Elizabeth Street. He wasn't Billy the Kid or one of the Daltons, prepared to shoot it out with a police station. He couldn't beat Captain Bart with a Glock or a Colt. He would come at Bart from the sea, like Sinbad the Sailor, and poison the waters around Bart. But there were no seas in the neighborhood.

And Isaac hadn't come in orange pants, pretending to be the wild man of Odessa.

No one handed him a crumpled dollar bill. No one called him El Señor. He was one more pol, a possible vice-president, and pols had no place in the badlands. He wandered around with Martin Boyle, drifted into that curious Sahara, where the sand was dark and wet.

"What are we looking for, sir?"

"I don't know."

And the Big Guy recovered all his wits. He saw three brats in filthy clothes circle a rock. They were laughing like hyenas. Their leader poked at something with a stick. Isaac stood on his heels, with a horrendous face, and clumped along like Frankenstein. The brats ran away from their rock.

"Ah," Isaac said, with a blend of bitterness and joy he couldn't have experienced anywhere outside the badlands. Raskolnikov was lying near the rock, only half alive. There was no illumination in the rat's eyes. He had blisters all over his body. His claws were gone.

Isaac picked up the rat, cradled him.

"Come on, Raskolnikov. We're going home."

13

Isaac found a vet who bathed Raskolnikov in a pink lotion, fed him dark milk in special baby bottles. The maid took pity on Raskolnikov and decided not to quit. She boiled the bottles. Raskolnikov sucked on a tiny nipple, but nothing seemed to happen until Marianna returned from a weekend with her mom and dad. The rat blinked at Marianna, and his eyes lit up with their usual suffering look. He started to chant. But Raskolnikov had lost that deep metallic timbre. He must have been mourning Dougy too much . . .

A giant in soiled pants marched through the gate, called himself Hernan Cortez. He was the last stoolie Isaac had on this earth. The Big Guy had rescued him from Rikers, where Cortez had been languishing without a number or a dossier. The system had "forgotten" Cortez, placed him in purgatory. Isaac discovered him on his annual walk through the City's jails. The Big Guy had a fondness for numberless men. Cortez was a gravedigger. He'd grown up in the Bronx, among the

Latin Jokers, but he'd never really been a Joker. Isaac had sent him out with a small party of men to find young Doug's remains. Cortez scoured the badlands with flashlights and shovels. The dirt of the Maldavanka was still on his face and pants. He watched Isaac feed Raskolnikov with a baby bottle.

"Boss, there were rats like him in Rikers. I taught them how to play a little violin."

Isaac didn't even look up from the bottle. "Raskolnikov's no prison rat. He's from the badlands . . . well, what do you have for me? A finger? An eye? Give Uncle Isaac the gruesome details."

"'S nothing to give. Boss, we searched everywhere. We shoveled up old bones, perfect, beautiful skeletons of dogs, cats, drug dealers, but there wasn't a fresh grave to be found. Mr. Doug isn't buried in the badlands, not the least part of him."

"How can you be so sure? Did you get into the cellar at Elizabeth Street?"

"We did." The ghoul winked at Isaac. "We posed as exterminators, had a permit . . . but Mr. Doug isn't under Bart Grossvogel's ground."

"I saw Dougy's blood in a dream . . . he has to be dead."

"You can't have a corpse without a corpus delicti . . . even in a dream."

"Ah," Isaac said, "you're a philosopher now."

"No, I dig and undig graves. And Mr. Doug doesn't have a grave, not yet. But I did hear the Latin Jokers rejoicing."

"Rejoicing? Where?"

"In that other badland. They were having a party on Featherbed Lane."

"And what the hell was Hernan Cortez doing at a Joker party?"

"I'm their mascot, their little homey, I do graves for them, get rid of the corpus delicti."

"They didn't mention Doug?"

"Not once."

"Then what was the rejoicing about?"

"Dunno. But they kept saying 'Sixteen hundred.' Sixteen hundred this, Sixteen hundred that."

"You're my scout, Hernan, and you don't even have a clue? What's the address of the White House?"

The ghoul shrugged his shoulders. "Dunno."

"Sixteen hundred Pennsylvania Avenue. The Jokers have a new sponsor. Calder Cottonwood."

Isaac dismissed the ghoul, sent him into the street with a butterscotch cookie. Then he collared Martin Boyle and Joe Montaigne.

"The Prez has to have a game plan. What is it?"

The two Secret Service men rocked on their heels.

"That's wise," Isaac said. "Dummy up. The Prez falls and falls in the pols. He's practically out of the race, but he sends a dying Bronx gang into the badlands with catchers' masks. He isn't senile. Laddies, what's his game plan?"

"Sir," Boyle said, "we're guarding you and Marianna. Calder doesn't trust us. We've been blipped off his screen. We're floating in space."

"How did he get to be Prez?"

"He kicked the shit out of the Democrats. He broke their ass."

"Then why isn't he breaking ass now?"

Isaac put the rat in a shoebox and went on the road with Marianna. He shunned auditoriums and sports palaces, kept away from the usual campaign trails. He visited junior high schools and nursing homes and hamlets that had a single soda fountain and general store. No one drummed for Isaac. He didn't have advance men. He would arrive unannounced, off the cuff, with sandwiches in his pockets and lettuce for Raskolnikov. He appeared at coffee klatches, dances, and bingo games, defying the conventional wisdom of Republicans and Democrats. He didn't go for the numbers, wasn't looking for the big score. But he and the little first lady electrified whoever they met. He was scoring in the heartland, converting people who had never voted in a national election. He was as dangerous to Tim as he was to the Prez. He was campaigning for the singular party of Isaac Sidel.

But Sinbad wasn't really fishing for votes. He wanted to draw Pamela Box into his little net. He could have phoned the White House. But the number-two man on the Democratic ticket wasn't supposed to confer with Calder Cottonwood's chief of staff. He thought of going back to Riverrun Estates, camping outside Ferdinand Antonescu's door. But Pamela would have read his motives, seen right through Sinbad. And so he campaigned with a rat in a shoebox, puzzled by Pamela, who hadn't come to pounce on him.

One afternoon, while he was trying on a pair of pants in a general store outside Philadelphia, Pam appeared. She was wearing a sexy leather outfit that seemed bold for a chief of staff.

She ducked under the little curtain and went right into the changing booth with Isaac. Sinbad was magisterial. He gave her a calculated kiss. And they rocked in the booth, completely naked, though Isaac had the devil of a time shucking off her leather pants.

"Pam," he whispered.

"Don't talk."

She hugged the ceiling while Isaac entered her. He looked into Pamela's eyes. They revealed what Isaac had already guessed. She wasn't afraid of him and his tricks. He watched her back in the mirror, the magnificent, muscular lines.

She nibbled his ear, got dressed, sneaked out of the booth, and Isaac wondered if the White House had planted cameras in the wall. She was smoking a cigarette when Isaac came out in his new pair of pants.

"Chinos," she said, "like a college freshman."

"They're practical. The seat doesn't wear out when you're rushing from place to place."

"And have to carry J. Michael. Because he's nothing in the polls without you."

"Why'd you come here, Pam?"

"I was curious . . . I wanted to taste you, Isaac dear. But not in an ordinary bed. That would have been banal."

"And how did I taste?"

"Like a Democrat about to lose an election."

"Pam, don't misjudge J. He can get very hot. And your man's been lying in a coma."

"He'll wake up faster than a baseball czar."

"Fine. And I'll carry J. if I have to. I've got a pretty broad back."

"I know. I was watching it while you were watching

— 131 —

mine . . . don't tell me I'm your new passion flower. What the hell do you want from the White House?"

"A whiff of reality."

"Reality? You're in the wrong business."

She glided out of the general store and into a black limousine, and vanished from Brighton, Pennsylvania, before the television crews following Isaac and the little first lady realized that Pam had ever been around. Isaac didn't budge from Brighton. He guarded the shoebox while Marianna phoned Gracie Mansion and talked to Alyosha for half an hour. He drank a Coke; half the population gathered outside the store. He collected Marianna, and with the shoebox under his arm, he chatted with different people in front of the cameras, behaved like a citizen with a new pair of chinos from the general store.

"Isaac, will you change America?"

"Ma'am, I was hoping America would change me."

"But how will you represent us?"

"Like I'm doing now. I'll listen . . . I'll buy another pair of pants next year. What else does a vice-president have to do?"

People clapped with the television cameras in Isaac's face.

"I'll travel around the country with Marianna Storm . . . when I can steal her from school. If I have to fight Congress, I will. If I have to argue with the President, I'll walk into the White House and whistle loud as I can."

He walked back inside the general store, while the population screamed, "Citizen, Citizen, Citizen Sidel."

Boyle whispered in his ear, "Sir, what the hell are we waiting for? You've conquered this tin can. Let's move on."

Isaac drank another Coke. He smiled when Tim Seligman

floated through the door with the biggest frown Isaac had ever seen on a man.

"Sidel, you're grounded, you hear? As of this moment, you are not traveling for the Democratic Party. We won't finance these little excursions. Damn you, J. Michael can't get any press while you and Marianna are on the road. You're eating into our prime time . . . what's inside that shoebox?"

"Dougy Knight's pet rat. I had nowhere else to keep him."

All the fire went out of Tim. He hid his face inside a handkerchief. "Do you realize what will happen to us if word leaks out that you and Marianna are campaigning with a rat?"

Isaac marched Timmy to an open stairway behind the store.

"The Prez had Dougy killed. I couldn't abandon his rat."

"Isaac, shut up. You can't accuse the President of killing people. We're in the middle of a campaign, or don't you remember?"

"I remember. But the Prez is losing points every day. Why doesn't he fight back?"

"He's licked, and he knows it."

"Licked, huh? He has the ammunition. He could attack J., talk about the phony land deals in the Bronx, the baseball czar who was getting ready to off his own wife."

"Calder's hands are tied. We arranged a quid pro quo."

"What *quid pro quo?*"

"We have the goods on him . . . photographs, tapes. Calder with all his bimbos."

"Including Margaret Tolstoy."

"Yes," Timmy said, excited now. "Including Margaret."

"And how did you get these tapes?"

"I can't reveal my sources. That wouldn't be ethical."

"Come on, Timmy, you're talking to the old Commish. You danced a little with the FBI. You cut a deal with the Bull, promised to keep him on during Michael's presidency. Bull supplied you with the tapes."

"No comment."

"Jesus," Isaac said. "You're a babe in the woods, and you're running the Democratic show."

"Stop that."

"The Bull is Calder's man. If he traded with you, it was Calder who told him to trade . . . how can you hurt the Prez? He has a couple of lollipops, so what? He's a widower, for God's sake. The country will sympathize with him. All you have on him is cock-a-doodle."

"And how would you know?" Timmy said, rocking on the back stairs.

"I looked into Pamela's eyes."

"Where? When?"

"She was in Brighton two hours before you. We made love behind a curtain . . . in the general store."

"Sidel," Timmy said, "are you criminally insane? Fucking the Prez's chief of staff?"

"That's not the point. I told you. I looked into her eyes. She isn't afraid of us. She's laughing her heart out."

"I'll meet with the National Committee. We'll pull you from the ticket, force you to resign."

Isaac drew Tim close, kissed him on the forehead. "Sweetheart, I'm the only weapon you have left."

14

Isaac returned to Gracie with his little caravan. Alyosha hadn't been idle. He was painting walls again, beyond the sanctuary of Carl Schurz Park. He abandoned Isaac as the object of his art, drew young Doug without a beard or a beret, and scribbled underneath, BENYA LIVES. Someone must have been feeding him tales about the Black Sea. *Benya Lives.* Dougy's corpse had disappeared, but he rose up on Alyosha's walls.

The murals troubled Isaac. He collected his chauffeur and crisscrossed Manhattan until he found the muralist.

"Homey, there's a price on your head."

Alyosha stood on a makeshift ladder with crayons in his fist, coloring the eyes of a dead man. Dougy had purple eyeballs in the drawing. Alyosha was on a hill in Washington Heights. Isaac snatched him *and* the ladder.

"Uncle, it isn't fair. I have work to do."

"I can see," Isaac said, staring at Mr. Doug on an abandoned, broken wall. "And who told you about Dougy's fate?"

"Bernardo."

"Bernardo's busy with Clarice."

"He always has time for a Joker."

"Wonderful," Isaac said.

Mullins drove them back to Gracie, but Isaac didn't get out of the car.

"Uncle, you abandoning me?"

"Have to visit your old gang, find out what happened to Benya's body."

"Take me," Alyosha said. "Uncle, I'm lonely for the Bronx."

"They'll tear your heart out and toast it like a marshmallow."

"I like marshmallows," Alyosha said.

Isaac dismissed his chauffeur. Mullins had a weak heart. The Big Guy crossed the Madison Avenue Bridge on his own and entered Joker country. He parked on Featherbed Lane. He wore his Glock high on the hip to show that he wasn't concealing a weapon, but no one seemed to care. Featherbed Lane was full of Glocks.

Isaac marched into the Jokers' clubhouse, a deserted dental clinic. Five or six Jokers fell on him.

"Maricón," they said, "you're not our mayor. What are you doin' here?"

"Sixteen hundred," Isaac said.

"Puta, that's not the password."

"Yes it is. You finished Doug, dragged him uptown. What did you do with his body? Donate it to Sixteen hundred Pennsylvania Avenue?"

"Big Balls, that bandido cop protected Angel Carpenteros. He wouldn't duel with us. He had to die."

"Where's his body?"

"He was a hero," the Jokers said. "We don't mutilate heroes. We wrapped him up and buried him in Valhalla."

"What Valhalla?"

"The bottom of the Hudson River."

"I don't believe you," Isaac said.

"Maricón, you can't call us liars in our own little mansion. You're just as guilty as the cop. Angel Carpenteros is your protégé."

"And I'm proud of it. Should I cry?"

These ferocious boys stared at Isaac. They looked undernourished in their rotting clubhouse-clinic. Isaac had a terrific desire to feed them butterscotch cookies.

"Puta," they said, "we'll make you cry."

They pummeled Isaac with their fists. But they hadn't counted on a mayor who loved to battle. The Big Guy was a brawler. He knocked one Joker on his ass, bit another Joker's ear. "Homeys, you'll need your catchers' masks. Let's play ball."

A sadness suddenly gripped Sidel. The boys he was fighting were only refugees. Isaac's own policemen had decimated the gang. But he shouldn't have grown sentimental in such a narrow space. The last of the Jokers, six boys, pulled out their Glocks.

"Big Balls, we'll count to three."

The Jokers never had a chance to count. A whirlwind arrived, knocked them against the wall, slapped the Glocks out of their hands. It was Bernardo Dublin, the nominal head of a gang he'd betrayed and betrayed.

The Jokers began to squeal. "Bernardo, you shoulda told us that Big Balls was on your list."

"He's the mayor. Show him a little respect."

"But he called us liars. This isn't Manhattan. It's Featherbed Lane."

Isaac had to hide his tears with his own hands. The little assassins would go on worshiping Bernardo until he betrayed them all.

"Bernardo," Isaac said, "it's a case of corpus delicti. Your homeys insist that Dougy Knight is at the bottom of the river. I don't believe them."

Bernardo grabbed two of the Jokers. "You heard the Big Guy. What did you do with Doug?"

"Bernardo, we wanted to bury him. But the feds raided our mansion. They dropped some money on us and grabbed Mr. Doug. 'Regards from Sixteen hundred.' That's all they told us."

"And you never reported the news to me?"

"How could we snitch on the President's people?"

"Homeys, who's the one and only president you'll ever have?"

"Bernardo Dublin."

Bernardo walked out of that cave with Isaac Sidel. "Boss, should I try and steal Dougy back?"

"Nah. It's too late. But how the hell did you know I was here?"

"Rembrandt paged me."

"Alyosha?"

"He worries about you. He says you can't even hold onto your pants."

✻   ✻   ✻

Isaac couldn't seem to function in a mayor's public house. He longed for his old apartment on Rivington Street, at the edge of the badlands. It was the Citizen's personal and private address.

He grabbed the shoebox and stole away from his mansion without the Secret Service, hitched a ride down to the Lower East Side like the famous vagabond that he was. Sidel. He had holes in his pockets, but he still had the right key to Rivington Street. He arrived at the tenement, walked up the stairs, and had a curious premonition that he wasn't alone. He turned the key in the lock, shoved at the door, and let Raskolnikov out of the shoebox. The rat hopped onto his shoulder. His tail was twitching. That was the only barometer Isaac needed. He pulled out his Glock. But a hand shoved at him with the force of a crowbar. He dropped the gun. He had a fist in his face. His ass was on the floor, but the rat was still curled around his neck.

"Raskolnikov," Isaac shouted, "will ya do something? Show your fucking claws." And then he realized who his assailant was. Raskolnikov wouldn't attack Doug's own dad.

Captain Knight was standing over Isaac.

"Hope you wouldn't mind, Mr. Mayor, if I borrowed your apartment."

"I didn't kill him, Cap."

"But you know who the murderers are, and you've done nothing about it."

"It's an election year, and—"

The captain kicked him in the chest.

The rat still clung to Isaac. "Latin Jokers. They were wearing catchers' masks."

"Masks, Mr. Mayor? But whose hands were behind those masks?"

"Barton Grossvogel. He stole—"

"Small potatoes."

He bent down, and Raskolnikov climbed onto him. "That's a good lad. Did you know that I was there, Mr. Mayor, the afternoon Dougy found the rat? It was uncanny. He looked up at us, like he was engaging us in a conversation. We fed the little starving bastard. And he was Dougy's for life . . . wouldn't leave his shoulder. And don't think he was domesticated. The beast is as wild as they come. A killer rat. But he must have felt a kinship with Doug. Coup de coeur. That's what Daniella would have called it. Thunder in the heart. I have thunder, Mr. Mayor. But it's a different kind. And it doesn't come from loving."

"Captain . . ."

"They went back on their word. Didn't I move to Arizona like a good little boy? And they butchered Doug."

"But he was supposed to leave the badlands."

"How could he leave when Bart Grossvogel turned the territory into his own random harvest? A man has a conscience, doesn't he?"

"Why did you bargain with them?"

"And what would you do, Isaac, when the President talks to you on the telephone, makes a personal appeal, and Bull Latham backs him up? It wasn't a lie. Dougy had been shooting people. He was indictable. I went along with their scheme . . . God, they must have chopped my boy into little pieces and hid them in a hundred empty orchards."

"He wasn't buried in the badlands."

"How do you know?"

"I had a team of gravediggers comb every orchard. They couldn't find Doug."

"So what? Your gravediggers stink."

Isaac didn't mention the other gravediggers, those from Sixteen hundred Pennsylvania Avenue. He didn't want to complicate his own little war with the White House.

The captain took Raskolnikov and returned him to Isaac's shoulder. "I'd keep him, but I have to travel light. And you'll need his companionship, you sorry son of a bitch."

The captain left Isaac sitting on his ass, and rushed out the door. Isaac went back uptown. The apartment didn't seem his anymore. It was someone else's lair.

He slept on the porch, drank Marianna's lemonade. He was no vengeance artist. He couldn't ruin Calder and the Bull with one masterful stroke, not while Bart was entrenched in his captain's castle on Elizabeth Street . . . and Anastasia was floating on Pennsylvania Avenue. Then fate seemed to sound in Isaac's ear. The President was coming to the Waldorf, would stay in his suite, and had scheduled a trip to the badlands, where he'd deliver an important speech. Isaac called J. Michael's headquarters, couldn't locate Bernardo Dublin. Bernardo could rescue him from the Jokers. That was kid stuff. Featherbed Lane. He called Clarice, but she was out somewhere with her bodyguard. Isaac left a message. She didn't return the call.

But he was Sinbad the Sailor. Clarice came to him, brought Bernardo along. "This mansion is worse than a bordello."

"What the hell do ya mean?"

"You turn a blind eye, let my little bitch of a daughter go to bed with a delinquent."

"Alyosha? Christ, he and Marianna are twelve years old."

"Almost thirteen."

"So they fool around a little."

"And I suppose you supervise all their play?"

Marianna appeared, hugging Alyosha's hand. "Mother, will you please go home."

"Bernardo," she said, "I command you to kidnap her."

Bernardo scratched his red mustache. "Ah, Clarice."

Isaac let Raskolnikov out of the shoebox, and while Clarice shrieked and ran behind an upholstered chair, he led Bernardo out to the porch.

"She's a handful, boss. She doesn't let me out of her sight. I had to duck her like a little devil to pull you out of the Bronx."

"Well, you'll have to duck her again and organize a posse."

"What's the posse for?"

"To keep Calder Cottonwood from getting killed."

Bernardo laughed with his Latin-Irish eyes. He was handsome as a movie star, but he couldn't have sat still long enough to perform in any film. Isaac mentioned the Maldavanka.

"Where's that?"

"The badlands between Catherine Street and Corlears Hook. Where Dougy died. Calder's gonna visit. And he might get glocked."

"By whom?"

"Captain Knight."

"And I drop the captain for you?"

"No. You surround him, keep him away from the Prez. But you don't hurt him, hear?"

"How do I hire people?"

"You can borrow all the men you want from my own detail."

"And what's my reward?"

"Gratitude," Isaac said.

Bernardo smiled. Isaac would never recruit another cop like Bernardo Dublin. They went back inside the house. Raskolnikov had already charmed Clarice. The rat was performing miracles. He carried matches on his whiskers, built a crooked teepee. Clarice clapped her hands. Marianna was feeding her vodka gimlets from the mansion's fridge.

Clarice was cockeyed. "Sinbad," she said, "did you tempt my bodyguard?"

And she began to snore on Isaac's couch, cradled in her own arms.

15

It was the Calder Cottonwood Show. Isaac couldn't compete with the flimflam of a president who hadn't left the White House in a month. The pollsters said he was sitting in his own grave. Calder hadn't even gone to his summer cottage. And then he came out of nowhere like a comet with a deep, presidential grin. He was six feet four, and during his honeymoon year on Pennsylvania Avenue Republicans looked at his profile and called it Lincolnesque. But he quarreled with his own cabinet, had to fire his first two chiefs of staff, and was soon a listless, unpopular president. He hired Pam, and she set about to undo all the damage.

He arrived at JFK on *Air Force One*, carrying the model of an enormous housing development, which his own architects, magicians in dark suits, assembled in Continental's first-class lounge. "A city within a city . . . like the Waldorf," he said. "But my city won't be for the superrich. I'm going to rip the heart out of the worst slum in Manhattan. I've spent sixteen months weeding out the pestilence in that jungle . . . and in other jungles across the land. But Manhattan is my baby. Isn't it where the twentieth century began? On an obscure patch lying in the bay. Ellis Island. How many of our grandpas poured into Manhattan from that immigrant station? Some went to Chicago. And St. Louis. But we'll start here, in *Century Town*. And I promise you. It won't have any second-class citizens. Affordable housing with a luxury look. We'll landscape it, build gardens . . . may I have a glass of water, please? I'm a little dizzy."

And he disappeared, popped up again in his motorcade, with Secret Service men on the trunk of his car, blocked traffic for three hours, brought mayhem to Manhattan as he slipped into the garage of the Waldorf Towers, and rode up to the Presidential Suite with Pamela Box wearing red, white, and blue.

He called Gracie Mansion, wanted Isaac to ride with him into the Maldavanka, help him christen Century Town as a bipartisan project, a Republican dream in a Democratic village. But Isaac didn't take the call. His deputies panicked. Calder Cottonwood had managed to co-opt Isaac Sidel, turn him into a struggling little boy.

Tim Seligman left a message. *Sidel, don't you dare ride down with that prick.*

Isaac needed counsel. But he had no one. His single network was a rat and two kids. He ran out of his mansion, summoned his chauffeur, and rode across the Verrazano Bridge to a posh insane asylum on Arthur Kill Road. He was visiting Becky Karp, the former mayor, who was in the middle of a monster depression. She'd torn out all her hair and had attempted suicide twice.

It was Isaac who'd committed her. She had no living relatives, and she'd become Isaac's ward. They'd been lovers once, when Isaac was the First Deputy Police Commissioner and Rebecca Karp ruled City Hall, an ex–beauty queen, Miss Far Rockaway of 1947. It was before Margaret Tolstoy had come back into his life. Becky fought with everyone, but she had an infallible instinct for things outside herself.

She wore a wig. Isaac could barely recognize her. Miss Far Rockaway had lost fifty pounds. She was skin and bones. But her depression seemed to lift.

"That cocksucker," she said. "Isaac, he wants to build his own model city in *our* town."

"I could sabotage his plans. He can't get a permit without me."

"Don't be ridiculous. You'll have to go along with him. He's won the round."

"But it'll look like I'm pimping for the Republican Party."

"No. We'll run circles around Calder Cottonwood. Help me get dressed."

"Why?"

"Schmuck, we're riding together in Calder's motorcade."

"But I can't release you, Becky. I don't have the power. We'll need an examining psychiatrist, and . . ."

"Isaac, it's simple. Pronounce me cured. Somebody's gotta believe you."

Isaac waltzed her past the reception desk, but a doctor stood in his way.

"Mr. President, sir, Rebecca isn't stable."

Isaac glared at the doctor's name tag. "Johnson, it's a matter of life and death. I have to consult with Her Honor. And I can't do it here. I'll bring her back. I promise."

The doctor looked into Isaac's eyes, saw the urgency and the madness. He wanted to straitjacket the two mayors, but he had to let them go.

"Thanks, Johnson, you won't regret it. I'll have a peek at your budget, and . . ."

"Please, sir, get the hell out of here."

They rode back across the Verrazano Bridge, Becky mesmerized by the burnt orange pillars.

"Isaac, wasn't that old bridge blue?"

"Never," Isaac declared. "Why did Calder keep mentioning Ellis Island? The whole country hates New York."

"But the country doesn't hate you. That cocksucker is trying to leapfrog onto your back."

They stopped at the Waldorf. Isaac paged the President from the Waldorf Towers desk. "Sidel here. I'd like to come up." Two Secret Service men in dark glasses accompanied him and Becky to the Presidential Suite. Pam met them at the door, whispered in Isaac's ear. "Who's the skeleton? Mrs. Death?"

Isaac ignored her and marched with Becky into the master bedroom, where the Prez was sprawled out on a four-poster that could barely accommodate his legs. He didn't scoff at Rebecca Karp.

"Hello, Madam Mayor," he said. "Good to see you again." He rose out of bed to offer her a seat in a black rocking chair. "That's the Kennedy rocker. It's priceless. Only three other chairs like it in the world. I do my best thinking in that chair."

Then he sat down again and summoned Isaac to the four-poster. "You're the Commish. Tell me, did the Kennedys have Marilyn killed?"

"Anything's possible, Mr. President."

Calder winked at Rebecca Karp. "He talks like a politician. Won't commit himself. But I think it's a shame. Both brothers boffing her, Jack and his little attorney general. Never liked Bobby. She was a *generous* girl, a schizophrenic princess. They broke her heart."

"Mr. President," Pam said, "do you have to keep talking about poor Marilyn Monroe?"

Calder grabbed a book from his night table and tossed it at Pam. She might have lost an eye if one of the Secret Service men hadn't deflected the book.

"Let's get down to details," she said. "Isaac, where will you ride? At the back of the motorcade?"

Isaac stared at Becky Karp. "With you," he said.

"That's impossible. We can't have Calder and a Democrat in the same car. People . . ."

The President glared at her. "Shut up. I like it. A couple of pioneers. Cottonwood and Sidel."

"And Becky Karp," Isaac said. "Becky rides with us."

"I'll buy that too . . . Mr. Mayor, I'm falling in love with your town. We'll take that goddamn slum and turn it into some hell of a garden."

Becky rocked in JFK's chair. "Calder," she told him, "cut the crap. That garden of yours is a fable. No government could ever afford it. You came into our yard and caught us with our pants down. Bravo. We have to go through the fiction that Isaac is going to help you build Shangri-la. We sit together, we smile . . . and then we go back to knocking each other's brains out."

"I love this girl," the President said. "Isaac, you're a lucky bastard. I could steal her from you and make her my Secretary of War."

"Mr. President," Pam said, "we don't have a Secretary of War. You mean Secretary of Defense."

"No," Calder said, smiling at Becky Karp. "I mean War."

They traveled down Fifth Avenue in the President's enormous limo, with Secret Service men on the roofs. Calder sat between Becky and Isaac, crossed his hands over his head like some heavyweight champion.

They arrived in the badlands, bumped across broken streets, crowds gathering behind them. The limo stopped in a burnt-out field, where Barton Grossvogel stood with his men, wearing parade uniforms. He saluted the Prez with a crisp white glove. And Calder's scenario began to make sense. Ah, Isaac mused like some downtown Hamlet, an amnesiac who was suddenly waking up. The fuckers couldn't afford to have Dougy around. Dougy would have spoiled their celebration, with his orange pants. A rogue cop who was protecting a district Calder wanted to claim as his own.

Isaac helped Becky out of the car. She could feel the mayhem under his skin. She shoved him along, steered him to the President's blind side. "Steady. You'll ruin us if you explode."

"But he'll make a fucking hero out of Bart."

"We'll unhero him . . . when the time is ripe. Control yourself."

"I can't."

"Isaac, if you're a sissy, I'm going back to Staten Island."

"Stay," Isaac said, "stay," and he joined Calder, Pam, and Bart, with a killer's smile. He couldn't find Bernardo Dublin. And for a moment he wished that Captain Knight would appear and get rid of Calder. But the Prez was inside a knot of Secret Service men. Isaac himself was part of that knot. He fingered the medals that covered Captain Bart's coat.

"Your Honor, I earned every one."

"I'll bet you did . . ."

Calder held out his arms, beckoned Isaac and Captain Bart.

"Good people," he said, his words riding the hot wind. "I'm not a shirker. I didn't summon you to some barren plain so you could hear an idle song. I intend to build. But we couldn't have had the idea without Bart Grossvogel, the captain who presides over this territory. You're standing on what was once a robbers' den. And Bart cleaned all the robbers out. He's my rabbi in Manhattan . . . along with Isaac Sidel."

Isaac began to sink inside his suit. Citizens from the Maldavanka stared at him as if he'd betrayed the Democratic donkey. "Isaac," an old woman mumbled to him. "Isaac, have you lost your mind?"

The Prez babbled about all the secular cathedrals he would put up on the downtown plains. And soon the Maldavanka had become a bit of Kansas and Nebraska. Reporters hounded Isaac, begged him for an interview.

"Children," he said, "it's Calder's day. Why should I steal from him?"

He was watching the streets when Bernardo Dublin appeared in dark glasses and roller blades. "Boss, if Captain Knight's around, he must be an invisible man."

Photographers snapped Isaac with the Prez. Becky clutched Isaac's hand. "Sonny, finish what you started. We ride uptown with him to the Waldorf."

Isaac grew more and more sullen as they drove out of the badlands. Pam dangled the President's cellular phone at him. "Tim Seligman. It must be urgent if he's calling you on the President's line."

Becky grabbed the phone. "Seligman, you can't disturb the Citizen. He's thinking." And she tossed the phone into Pamela's lap.

The Prez wouldn't go back into the secrecy of the Waldorf Towers. He strode up the Park Avenue stairs and entered the main lobby with Isaac Sidel, mingling with guests as the Secret Service formed a tightening circle around him. But he broke through the circle, waltzed with a bride who was on her honeymoon at the hotel. He'd come out of his month-long hibernation, and was eager to talk and dance. Isaac stared at the Secret Service men with their shades and button mikes, and he started to smile. One of them was much beefier than the rest, wore a suit that didn't seem to fit . . . and carried a Glock in his pants, like Sinbad himself. It was Captain Knight. Isaac didn't wait for the glint of that gun. He leapt into the air, tackled the President and the Waldorf bride, and caught a bullet in the slightly padded shoulder of his suit. The bride screamed. Guests dropped to the floor, hid behind furniture, as Secret Service men bumped into each other trying to shield the President. Captain Knight had already vanished in the hurlyburly.

Isaac pulled out his Glock. There was blood on his shoulder. He wasn't going to shoot Captain Knight. He wanted to save him from the Secret Service. He ran through a door into the bowels of the Waldorf, where the kitchen was located. He could have been dreaming. He'd stumbled upon some cooking school. He saw ten or fifteen chefs in white toques, with whipped-cream guns in their hands, working on a pile of pastry. The kitchen didn't seem to have an end. It was bigger than the Waldorf.

"Gentlemen," he said, "did a man in dark glasses come your way?"

The chefs looked at him with a certain pity in their eyes.

"Mr. Mayor, you're bleeding."

He marched back upstairs to the lobby. The President sat in a gilded chair. The Waldorf's chief physician rushed over to Isaac, cut away his shoulder pad with a pair of surgical scissors.

"Ah," Isaac said, "it's just a scratch," and saw black spots in front of his eyes.

16

The bullet had nicked his arm without entering Isaac. He wouldn't go to the hospital. He was given the Cole Porter Suite, where the same doctor dressed Isaac's wound. The Waldorf was receiving hundreds of calls. Isaac's own fate was like a maddening balloon. In a couple of hours he'd gone from being a turncoat to a champion who'd risked his own life to rescue Calder Cottonwood. The pollsters' new dream ticket was Cottonwood-Sidel, as if the nation wanted a president and vice-president outside the usual noise of political parties.

Sidel had destabilized the whole fucking process. He was like a force majeure, beyond energy fields. No one could tame him, except Rebecca Karp, who'd been hustled back to her asylum on Arthur Kill Road, while Isaac snored in Cole Porter's bed. What was it like to live for twenty-five years in a hotel that could have been an Art Deco battleship? Isaac fiddled with Porter's biography in his sleep, remembered a man who fell off a horse, crushed both his legs, became a cripple who couldn't walk without a pair of canes, but still traveled around the world from his suite at the Waldorf. Isaac had grown up on Cole Porter's songs, would have given his Glock to the devil if he could have written "Begin the Beguine."

He was like *another* president. The Waldorf had sewn his initials on his towels and bathrobe. He called the Arthur Kill asylum. "Becky, I didn't mean to abandon you . . ."

"Don't apologize. I had enough excitement to keep me going for a year. Careful, Isaac. You're swimming in a sea of sharks."

"But what if I don't swim?"

"They'll still eat you alive."

"I could get out of the race. Can't I retire in Cole Porter's bed?"

"Manhattan doesn't like losers. The Waldorf would kick you out on your ass."

But no concierge in white gloves appeared to present Isaac with a bill. He was the wounded warrior. He didn't have to campaign. He was on the covers of *Fortune* and *Vanity Fair*. With a scratchy face. Sinbad. He had fan clubs in forty-two states, and he still hadn't gotten out of bed. If he craved sausages, sausages would arrive, compliments of the chef. The Waldorf kitchen was open to Sinbad night and day.

He wished November would come without him, that he could shut his eyes and escape the elections. He told the Towers desk that he would only take calls from Marianna, Angel, and Rebecca Karp. His phone rang, and when he didn't recognize the voice right away, he growled, "Who is it?"

"Calder. Could you meet me at the Bull and Bear in twenty minutes? I'd be most grateful."

The Bull & Bear was a businessman's restaurant *inside* the Waldorf. Isaac didn't have to dress. He got into the elevator in his slippers and robe, like any invalid. It was past the lunch hour, and the restaurant had been closed off for the President, who stood at the eight-cornered mahogany bar in a linen suit, while Isaac stared at the Bull & Bear's electronic stock ribbon, even though he was an infant in matters concerning the market.

"I should have thanked you," Calder said. "Will you have a drink?"

Isaac didn't see one Secret Service man.

He had some lemonade. The Prez was clutching a glass of white wine. He blinked once, and the bartender disappeared. They were all alone in the Bull & Bear.

"It's no five-star restaurant," Calder said. "But I like the Caesar salad. Would you prefer to sit down?"

"No," Isaac said. "It's pleasant here." He could imagine Cole Porter sipping champagne at one of these eight corners.

"I'm spoiled. I feel like I own the place . . . that was Captain Knight, wasn't it? The mysterious stranger. Did he wing you on purpose? Was it a big act?"

"I doubt it, Mr. President. You had his son killed."

"I'm not going to spar with you, Sidel. The Service let me down. They should have spotted a lunatic in dark glasses, pretending to be one of their own . . . how'd he get away?"

"Through the kitchen. Ever been down there, Calder? It's like a military base."

"How are you sleeping, kid?"

"Like a prince. I have Cole Porter's bed."

"I can't sleep. I have nightmares. Margaret disappeared.

Not even Bull Latham can find her. Has she visited your suite? Because I'd give you the presidency if I can have Margaret back."

"Calder, did you get me out of bed to rub my nose in bullshit? Your men have been watching my door. Half the waiters who feed me work for you. I'll bet they're your poker partners on *Air Force One*."

"I can't live without Margaret."

Isaac left his lemonade on the Bull & Bear's mahogany. He got into his clothes. His hands weren't steady. He had the hotel barber shave him. He watched himself in the mirror. He was pale as a disinherited peach . . .

He didn't have much of a homecoming. His deputies weren't around. Marianna must have been in the park with her muralist. He couldn't find Boyle or Joe Montaigne. He climbed up to his bedroom and looked into a pair of silver-pink eyes.

"Raskolnikov," he said, "Raskolnikov."

But the rat wouldn't jump, wouldn't cling to Isaac's neck. He stayed on the pillow. And Isaac didn't have a single ally left.

17

The Big Guy couldn't sleep away from the Waldorf. He wanted to borrow Cole Porter's bed. Finally he drifted into a dream that was neither night nor day. Isaac had entered some curious zone where he was like a visitor at the movies, watching battles inside his head. The eyeless sailor appeared. Sinbad. He was harpooning someone, digging at him ferociously. Isaac heard a scream, recognized the sailor's victim. It was Isaac himself.

He got up from his couch, drank a glass of water, fed Raskolnikov. He understood the *rightness* of Sinbad's red harpoon. They meant to kill him. Calder and his gang. And the killer would be someone close to Sidel. He was sure of it.

He could join Becky in her asylum, put a couple of rivers between him and the assassins, whoever they were. And then the assassins announced themselves. Bull Latham had arrived with Captain Grossvogel, Clarice, and Bernardo Dublin.

"No more monkey business," Clarice said, after the Bull

brought Marianna down from her bedroom. "I have a judge's writ. I came to collect my little girl."

Marianna struggled in Clarice's arms, while Alyosha stood on the stairs.

"Wouldn't interfere," the Bull said to Isaac. "Am I wrong, Bart? You'd have to arrest our candidate for meddling with the law."

"But it was Clarice who lent Marianna to me."

"Lent," Bart sang, "that's the crucial word. And now the lender wants her back."

Marianna started to cry. "Uncle Isaac, don't let them take me. I'll only return to you and Alyosha."

"That reminds me," Bart said. "We have another writ. Seems that your little man has run away from a bad boys' hotel in Peekskill. We'll have to collect him too."

And he plucked Alyosha off the stairs. Isaac lunged at Bart, but Bernardo barreled into him. "Boss," he whispered, "they'd love to wallop you." And he abandoned Isaac, left with Clarice, Bart, the two kids, and Bull Latham.

The mansion was like a morgue. Isaac would ramble around, wondering if his maid, Miranda, had poisoned his food. Should he fire his whole fucking staff, camp out at Gracie like Robinson Crusoe? He could feel a red harpoon dig into his side. The mayor had lost his marbles.

He had to beg Raskolnikov to climb back into the shoebox. Took him an hour to coax the rat. Then he ran to the badlands with the box, returned to Rivington Street. He went to his old apartment, figuring he could chew the fat with Captain Knight. Where else did a renegade have to hide? But Isaac had picked the wrong captain. It was Captain Bart who waited for him on Isaac's sofa, Bart and two of his men with pump guns that could have dropped a bear. Isaac almost smiled. His dreams hadn't betrayed him. The red harpoon was there. And Isaac could identify this false Sinbad.

"Well," Bart said, "if it isn't our own little dear? I'm out of breath, love. Should the lads tell you how I raced to Rivington Street? Were you looking for Captain Knight? We just missed him or we would have blown his brains out. The nerve of that man. Trying to massacre our president. And you're the little hero, aren't you, love? Stepped between Calder and the bullet. But you had an advantage over us. You knew that Captain Knight was coming to the Waldorf. Made us look like imbeciles . . . Isaac, can you recollect a couple of prayers? You'll need them. Because Calder gave us the green light. Now he never said, 'Kill Isaac.' But he intimated that your health wasn't a concern of his. That you could disappear from the planet, and he wouldn't cry his eyes out . . . do you have anything to say? I'm interested in your last words."

"You shouldn't have swiped those catchers' masks."

Bart winked at his men. "He's practically dead and he thinks of stupid shit. What catchers' masks?"

"The ones you handed to the Latin Jokers."

"Indeed. I stole the idea from you and your Delancey Giants."

"Did I ever harm you, Bart, when I was the Commish?"

"Not at all. But we were in the same class at the Academy. And I watched you rise and rise like a great big ball of fire, while all the Irish chiefs fed your flame."

"You weren't in my class. I would have remembered."

"That's just it. I didn't stick out. I had to grub my way. I had to fight in the dark. And someone's got to suffer. Why not you?"

He leaned forward with all his bulk and cracked Isaac. Blood spurted onto the ceiling. Isaac had a split lip, but he still clutched the shoebox. One of Barton's boys attacked Isaac's legs with the long nose of his pump gun. Isaac tripped, banged into a lamp; the bulb shattered under the shade.

"What's he holdin' on to, Bart? Is he a miser? Does he have money in that box?"

Bart whacked him again. Blind figures appeared in front of Isaac's eyes, like so many Sinbads. But they weren't carrying spears. They were stumbling, like Sidel. They could have been the bits and pieces of his personality. "Mothers," he cried, "I don't know who I am."

Barton nudged his boys, laughed. "He's going out like a winner, isn't he, lads?"

"Where should we dump him, Bart?"

"Right here. Let him bleed to death in a dry tub. The coroner will call it suicide."

"That's brilliant, Bart."

Isaac opened the shoebox. Raskolnikov swirled into the air, scratched Barton's eyes, bit off half his nose, while his two accomplices stood like stone men. Isaac kicked the pump guns out of their hands, socked them into a little alley behind the sofa. He could feel Raskolnikov near his neck. Barton sat on the floor, clutching the remains of his nose.

"Next time, Bart, don't brag so much when you want to kill a man."

Isaac called an ambulance, but he didn't wait. Bart could attend to himself, explain what he was doing in Isaac's apartment with a pair of pump guns and half a nose . . .

Isaac had a guest when he got to the mansion gate. The Butcher of Bucharest with all his belongings. Shopping bags, books, a little valise.

"Ah," Isaac said, "did you use up Alexandria, Uncle Ferdinand? Margaret's missing, and Calder took his revenge, locked you out of that fancy nursing home the Bureau has for senile double agents."

"I ran away . . . with Margaret's help."

"Margaret's in Manhattan?"

"More or less. She promised you would take me in."

"I ought to drown you."

"It's been tried. But I grow gills when I'm under the water. How else could I have survived the Black Sea?"

Isaac had no answer. He led Ferdinand into Gracie with the shopping bags and the little valise.

They were like a couple of bears. They watched television, played chess. Isaac wouldn't fall asleep around Ferdinand. He should have locked the Butcher inside one of the bedrooms, but he couldn't be brutal to a houseguest. He slept with Raskolnikov on his blanket. The rat was enough of an alarm.

And after Ferdinand's fifth night in the mansion, Isaac relaxed a bit. He shared a big pot of chocolate sorbet from Bloomingdale's. Isaac whistled in his sleep, woke with his arms and legs strapped to an antique chair in his own bedroom. Raskolnikov wasn't on the bed.

Ferdinand stood near the fireplace. The room was full of

smoke. That son of a bitch was building a fire on a hot September day.

"How did you break in? There's a combination lock on the door . . . it's impregnable. No burglar could have mastered that lock."

"But I'm not a burglar, Monsieur. And your little lock was child's play."

"Where's Raskolnikov? You shouldn't be alive."

"I was a familiar face. You let me near your rat. I bagged him. He's in his shoebox in the master closet."

"You spiked the sorbet."

"With a little sleeping powder. After all, I had to eat from the same batch. It was delicious."

He turned toward Isaac with a poker in his hand. It was red hot.

"Margaret didn't send you. You're the President's own package."

"Something like that," Ferdinand said. "I'm a torturer. You never lose the habit. What else can I do?"

"And you're going to burn my eyes out."

"Eventually," Ferdinand said. "But I'm an artist, Monsieur. I wouldn't go right for the eyes."

"You're not even looking for information."

"Information? You have nothing to give."

"Then you'll poke my eyes out for the fun of it, eh Ferdinand?"

Isaac should have wet his pants. His teeth should have chattered inside his head. But he couldn't figure out why he wasn't afraid.

"Are you ready, Sinbad?"

The poker grazed Isaac's chin. The heat was horrible. He heard a rustling noise. The poker flew into the air. Ferdinand yelped and screamed. Margaret Tolstoy had arrived in the long yellow hair of a mermaid. She knocked him silly with a single punch.

"You'll injure him," Isaac said. "He's an old man."

"Darling, I almost didn't get here in time."

"He's one more geek who wants to murder me. Calder is sending out assassins."

"Calder didn't send him. Ferdinand's freelancing. He broke out of Riverrun, figured he'd do a little mischief . . . I'm the assassin Calder sent."

She put out Ferdinand's fire. Then she straddled Isaac, kissed him while his hands were tied. And now he began to shake, because he'd never understood Margaret Tolstoy. Killing him or kissing him might come to the same thing. Perfect, endless rapture that only a man like Sinbad or Isaac Sidel could ever realize. Would she strangle him? She managed to lower his pants; she made love to him like an executioner, rode Isaac with her head pulled back, the mermaid's yellow hair in his eyes. Am I dead, he wondered? Good. I won't have to face the Democrats or the Republicans. But he'd miss Raskolnikov and Alyosha and Marianna Storm.

Margaret untied him.

"You're his only weakness," she said. "Can't you understand? Michael is nothing."

"Nothing in November?"

"Now or November. Nothing. Calder can't control himself. He's jealous of you. And he has no limits, darling. He's the President. He can bomb the Chrysler Building if he wants."

"But J. Michael is killing him in the polls."

"Not really, not without you as his running mate . . . but it isn't all political. He can't bear that we were childhood sweethearts. That *our* past is much deeper than his and mine."

"It's your fault," Isaac said. "You shouldn't have played Scheherazade with him, told him a fairy tale."

"Idiot. It's the only thing that kept you alive. Calder loved the details. And he has you licked. I promise."

"No. Michael will wake up."

"Darling, Michael's in the middle of a nightmare."

"Since when?"

"Since Bull Latham had a talk with him and Clarice. Two days after the Democratic Convention. If he wins or not, he'll never be sworn in. You know all about his phony land deals, but there's much, much more. He embezzled money from his own firm in Florida, or he and Clarice couldn't have stayed afloat. Marianna would have had to give up her private school . . . The hero of our time. The man who saved baseball. Isaac, he's in the Prez's pocket. He's going to throw the first debate."

"Michael's not a quitter."

"Darling, have you looked into his eyes lately?"

"He won't let me near him. He stole Marianna."

"To isolate you even further, make you the ghost of Gracie Mansion."

"And what about Dougy's ghost? Is it haunting Pennsylvania Avenue?"

"I buried Doug in the rose garden . . . at Riverrun."

"He's lying in Alexandria, among all the spooks?"

"Can you think of a better camouflage? No one will ever bother about Dougy's grave. Darling, it was the best I could do."

Isaac stared at the door of his closet. "God, I forgot."

He opened the closet door, let Raskolnikov out of the shoebox. The rat jumped onto his shoulder, looked at Margaret, but he wouldn't deliver his metallic squeal of love. This was only a mermaid, not Marianna Storm.

Part Five

18

Isaac had to get technical. It was the only way. He didn't have the firepower to declare war on the United States. He went downtown to the Microbe, his electronics maven. The Microbe had a shop on Liberty Street. He was choosy about his clientele. He was the best wiretapper in the business. Alfred Smart. That was the name on his birth certificate. He'd had his own lab before his managers at Westinghouse realized that he was freelancing for the Mafia . . . and maverick mayors like Isaac Sidel.

He never left his shop. He was like a pint-sized Tom Edison, a surly, pathological shrimp. But he adored Isaac. His window blinds were down. Isaac had to knock and knock. "Microbe, it's me."

Isaac stood there while iron bars began to screech. The Microbe had barricaded himself. The door opened. Isaac rushed in, and the Microbe, a decrepit young man still in his twenties, with the darkest circles around his eyes that Isaac had ever seen, slid the iron bars back into place.

"Alfred," Isaac said. "I need."

"Yeah. You're like a wild chicken in a shooting gallery."

"I need," Isaac muttered.

"Death is sitting on your shoulder. I can taste his stink. How can I help?"

"A bug," Isaac said, "a wire so magnificent, the Bureau couldn't shake it out of me."

"You want a bug that no one can find? . . . then keep away from wires. We go with a digital device. But I have to warn you. The sound isn't great. How near will you be to the target?"

"Nose to nose."

"Perfect. My baby has a range of two feet. And it only works indoors. The slightest breeze could kill it."

"Indoors, Alfred. A restaurant."

"With waiters hovering around?"

"I'll get the waiters to disappear. I'll do my werewolf number, snarl at them."

"Too much noise and baby starts to whistle."

"I don't need a Stradivarius, only a bug that's a little too clever for Bull Latham."

The Microbe stood up, poked through the debris behind him, and plucked out an alligator belt. He dangled the belt in front of Isaac. "Put it on."

Isaac removed his own belt, and put on Microbe's little baby. "That's genius. The device is right inside the buckle."

"Don't mock me, Isaac. Only a moron would use a buckle. My baby's sewn inside the skin."

"How do I trigger it?"

"Baby triggers herself. And if you wanna play back the conversation, you touch the metal tongue, and baby starts to purr."

"I'm worried. If Bull knows I've been here, will he start persecuting you?"

"Probably. But I have another shop around the corner. And he can't persecute me for too long. I supply the mutt with his best devices. His own shop stinks."

Isaac wiped his eyes with a handkerchief. Alfred tried to console him. "What's the matter?"

"You should be a billionaire, like Bill Gates. And you're stuck in a toilet on Liberty Street."

"Bill Gates, Bill Gates. Who could live in Seattle? It rains all the time."

"But it's beautiful, Alfred. I've been there. The coffee's terrific. You have mountains, seven hills, the sea. It's like living on top of the world."

"Me? I never travel."

Isaac returned to Gracie, called the FBI. "Sidel here. I'd like to speak to the Director."

"He isn't available at the moment, sir. Can I take a message?"

"Tell the Bull I love him. Good-bye."

Isaac whistled in his armchair, picked up a copy of Isaac Babel's *Odessa Tales,* and read about Benya Krik, king of the Maldavanka, who marries off his sister, Deborah, a forty-year-old virgin with a goiter problem, an enlarged gland that gave her a permanently swollen neck. The king invites every beggar in town to his sister's wedding. The police are about to raid the wedding party, capture Benya Krik, humiliate him in front of all the petty gangsters of the Maldavanka, congregating in their orange pants on Hospital Street. But the police never arrive. The king's henchmen set fire to their barracks, and they have to hurry home to put out the blaze. There was only one king of Odessa, Benya Krik . . .

The telephone rang. Isaac, absorbed in the story of gangsters on the Black Sea, and in his own Maldavanka near the Williamsburg Bridge, let the phone ring. Finally he growled into the receiver, "Sidel here."

"That was some message, Isaac. I'm the talk of the town. Telling my switchboard that you love me."

"Ah, it was only a little valentine, Bull. Among killers and friends."

"What the fuck do you want?"

"Meet me at the Bull and Bear in an hour."

"That's the Prez's watering hole. I can't invade his territory."

"The Bull and Bear."

"I'm in D.C., for Christ's sake."

"Baloney. You're in Manhattan. You've been assigned to me, Bull. I'm the cross you have to bear. Don't be late."

The Bull was already seated at a corner table when Isaac entered the restaurant from the Waldorf's lobby. He was signing autographs. No one seemed to forget his days on the Dallas Cowboys.

Isaac sat down. He was like a runt next to Bull Latham.

"You're wired, aren't you?" Bull said.

"You can frisk me. I'm not shy."

"It's hopeless. You've been to Alfred Smart. He could have

shoved a device inside your belly button. I'd have to carve out half your gut . . . by the way, I'm gonna arrest your rodent. That rat of yours chewed Bart Grossvogel's face."

"It's Dougy's rat, not mine. I had to adopt him. You shouldn't have killed young Doug."

"Speak a little louder, Sidel. Alfred's mikes are sensational, but they lack a certain mellowness of tone."

"You can dance with Tim Seligman, steal Marianna for Clarice, but it's a big act. You're the President's man."

"I'm neutral," Bull said with a smile.

"You're the President's man, and Tim's a fool. He can't even figure out that J. Michael's ready to hand the election to Calder. Did you scare the shit out of J.? Did you talk penitentiary to him and Clarice? They're a couple of children. But Sinbad's right behind them. And I'll run in Michael's slot if I have to."

"I'll bet you would."

"How much of a file do you have on me, Bull? Big as a telephone book?"

"Bigger. You've cohorted with the Maf, you've murdered people."

"But I never took a dime. America likes desperadoes. They'll call me Wild Bill Hickok or Wyatt Earp. I'll knock Calder into the ground . . . I'm a little crazy, Bull. You know that. I want you to get rid of Bart Grossvogel, shove his ass into the wind."

"Why would I do that?"

"Because if you don't distance yourself from him, you're gonna take a fall."

"Are you threatening me, Mr. Mayor?"

"Yes, Bull . . . did your microphones pick that up? I'll link you and him to Dougy's death."

"Captain Knight killed young Doug. Weren't you at the funeral?"

"You're an assassin, Bull."

"Are you going to complain about me to your police commissioner? I kind of like Sweets. I've worked with him on a few task forces."

Carlton Montgomery III, aka Sweets, had been a college basketball player, like Calder Cottonwood. His pa was a dentist, a black millionaire. He was the one man in America that Isaac was afraid of, his own PC.

"Barton's a crook," Isaac said.

"Sweets will never arrest him, kid. Calder couldn't have an anti-crime commission without Barton Grossvogel. And you're asking your PC to buck the President of the United States. Sweets isn't as suicidal as yourself."

"What happens when Captain Knight surfaces again? He'll have a pretty story to tell."

"He's a fugitive. He tried to kill the Prez. He'll be shot on sight. And I'd like to end this interview. I'm hungry. Can I buy you lunch?"

"Nah," Isaac said, looking at the Bull & Bear's eight-sided bar. He could have spent his life at this hotel, eaten here every afternoon, without Bull Latham. He'd fucked up, even with his alligator belt. He couldn't damage the Bull. They were laughing at him.

He called One Police Plaza from the lobby of the Waldorf. He had to hold the line. The Commish wouldn't talk to him right away. A concierge approached Isaac. "Will you be using your suite today, sir?"

He'd risen in the world, Sinbad-Sidel, who could move in and out of Cole Porter's bed. He muttered, "Yes . . . no . . . yes."

"Very good, sir. We'll put chocolate mints on your night table. And some fresh fruit."

Sweets jumped onto the line. "You can't come to One PP. You'll create a riot. Every cop in the building will want to shake your hand."

"Meet me at the Waldorf."

"Isaac, I have a press conference in—"

"Push it back. You're the Commish. I'll be waiting for you. In the Cole Porter Suite."

"Isaac, you're a downtown boy. What the hell are you doing at the Waldorf?"

"I live here . . . sometimes."

Sweets sat down at the piano, played Cole Porter for Isaac Sidel. He was six feet six and he had to tuck his legs under the piano bench.

"I want you to close Barton Grossvogel's shop," Isaac said.

"Fire me, Mr. Mayor. Find yourself a yes man. I'm not getting involved in your duel with the Prez."

"Bart's a gangster."

"I know . . . but I can't flop him right now. You'll compromise your own police department. The papers will call us Isaac's little boys. I'm not playing presidential politics . . . who the hell put him in the captain's chair at Elizabeth Street?"

Isaac shrugged his shoulders. "I can't remember."

"You did. It was the badlands. You wanted a rough cop. And the Prez picked Bart to bulldoze the area."

"With corpses lying in the ground."

"Who was his best soldier?"

"Young Doug."

"No. Margaret Tolstoy."

"She was on loan from the White House."

"Isaac, you can't have Bart without Margaret, White House or no White House. I shackle him, I shackle her. How does that sit with the future vice-president? . . . you brought me up here. Let me breathe in a little Cole Porter."

Isaac stood near the piano, and both of them sang "Begin the Beguine."

19

He slept at the Waldorf, had monstrous dreams. A rat with blond hair was swallowing his arm like a python or a whale. Sinbad woke in the middle of the night. He sucked on a chocolate mint, ate a peach. Nothing could console him.

He dressed at five in the morning, walked uptown to his mansion with the sun rising around him, the river at his feet. Tugboats recognized Sidel, signaled to him with their foghorns. It was like a serenade. No one could grab his city, not Calder, not the Bull. He panicked. He didn't want to live in D.C., have his own little office at the White House. But he had to avenge young Doug, or the ghosts of the Maldavanka would haunt him for the rest of his life.

Martin Boyle was waiting in the breakfast room.

"Boyle, did they let you out of the zoo?"

"Sorry, sir, I was on a bender."

"Where's Joe Montaigne?"

"With Marianna, sir."

"Pamela indoctrinated you, didn't she? She took away your brownie points, because you got a little too fucking close to Sidel. You're supposed to save my life *and* spy on me . . . Boyle, tell the truth, are you ready to break the law?"

"Yes, Mr. President."

"Will you kidnap Marianna for me?"

"With pleasure, sir. I can't survive without her cookies."

"Neither can I . . . do you know where Clarice is keeping her?"

"I can find out."

"From whom?"

"Joe Montaigne."

"He's loyal to us?"

"He always was, sir. But he's assigned to Marianna. He has to be near her body."

"And if I shut my eyes, Boyle, if I nap on the sofa, nod off for a couple of hours, because I feel like shit, will you wake me with a good surprise?"

"I'll do my best, sir."

And Isaac did nod off. He dreamt of a strange perfume. Butterscotch. He woke with a smile. Marianna was in the kitchen, with her baking gloves that looked like catchers' mitts. Joe Montaigne and Martin Boyle stood near the sink, like a company of dwarfs attending Snow White.

Isaac padded into the kitchen, hugged Marianna Storm.

"Darling," she said, "I can't bake *and* kiss."

"Sorry," Isaac said, "sorry."

"Why did you wait so long to rescue me? And where's Alyosha?"

Isaac let the rat out of the shoebox. Raskolnikov looked at Marianna and leapt into the air with a whistling love song.

"Ah, Alyosha," Isaac said. "We'll find him."

The guard telephoned from the gate. "There's trouble, sir. It's the Commish."

"Jesus," Isaac said. He coaxed Raskolnikov back into the shoebox and sent Marianna upstairs with Martin Boyle and Joe Montaigne to hide in the attic. He shut the door of the kitchen, but a butterscotch aroma had already invaded the house.

Sweets marched in and handed Isaac a sheet of paper. "I'm not covering for you. You have my resignation."

Isaac stuffed the paper into his mouth and started to chew.

"That's wonderful, a grown man eating a letter. But I can scribble another one, boss."

"Did the Bull send you?"

"Is that a crime? Since when is the Bureau outlawed in New York City?"

"He's the President's man."

"Shut up, or I'll handcuff you. I ducked the reporters, Isaac. I sneaked uptown, but if you can't produce Michael's little girl in twenty-four hours, I will have to arrest you and that pair of clowns who are with the Secret Service."

"Sweets, it's the only way I can get Michael to react."

"I told you, boss, shut the fuck up. How many times does Marianna have to get kidnapped in one campaign?"

"But she wants to live with me. She hates her mom and dad."

"Then plead for her at Family Court . . . where's the rodent?"

"What?"

"Isaac, you can't keep a rat as a pet. Do you want to start another bubonic plague?"

"Sweets, I swear, he's almost human. His name is Raskolnikov. He was young Doug's bodyguard . . . in the badlands."

"Shall I send for the exterminators, or will you give me the rat?"

Isaac took Raskolnikov out of the shoebox. The rat stared into Sweets' eyes, and the Commish had to grab himself or he would have shivered to death. The fucking rat had all the sadness of New York City in his eyes.

"Damn you," Sweets said, "put him back inside his cradle, and I'll forget I ever saw him. I don't want to have bad dreams. But if you can't produce the girl, I'm finished with you."

And Sweets left the mansion. Isaac brought his three fugitives down from the attic, and Raskolnikov danced between Marianna's legs.

"Where's Michael?"

"I'm not sure," Marianna said. "Mom can't bear to have him at Sutton Place. She's too busy with Bernardo Dublin."

"Could Bernardo find him for us?"

"I told you, darling. Mom's voracious. She can never get enough of Bernardo Dublin."

"Guys," Isaac said to Martin Boyle and Joe Montaigne, "is there a brothel he uses, or what?"

"Well," Joe Montaigne said, "I've tracked him a coupla times to Executive Suite . . . it's like the back door to the Rainbow Room . . . ya know, billionaires, hotshot politicians, chairmen of the board—"

"And J. Michael Storm. Where is it?"

"It's part of a health club at the Alhambra, a midtown hotel."

The phone rang. Sinbad grabbed the receiver. "Sidel here."

"You cocksucker. Don't move."

And J. Michael appeared at Isaac's door. He dismissed his retainer of Secret Service men, banished them to the porch.

"Sinbad the Sailor. You son of a bitch."

He socked Isaac in the mouth. And Sinbad landed on his ass again.

"Dad," Marianna said, "don't you dare hurt him."

"Baby, are you all right?"

And Michael started to cry. "I can't take the tension. I'll abdicate."

"Dad, you can't abdicate. You're not a king."

"You," he pointed to Isaac, "upstairs."

And they retreated to the little library on the second floor.

"You're an ingrate," Michael said. "I lend you my daughter, and then you steal her from me."

"J., I had to light a fire under your ass. I couldn't even get an interview with you. Do you know how many times I asked?"

"I'm campaigning, you prick."

"That's the problem," Isaac said. "You're not . . . the Bull has put you in Sleepy Hollow."

"What does that mean?"

"He's talked you and Clarice right out of the election."

"Isaac, get rid of your spies. They stink."

Sinbad seized Michael's collar. "I could strangle you. I wouldn't mind a prison term. I'd welcome it . . . J., you were the best. I was proud of you, even when I was a policeman on the other side of the barricades. The whole country watched you on the tube . . . you read from Spinoza, John Donne. You said that education wasn't an instrument of national policy . . ."

"Isaac."

"That words themselves were part of the revolution."

"It was centuries ago, in sixty-eight."

"That's the problem. We're moving backwards all the time. If we're not careful, we'll be bumping into another Stone Age."

"You can afford to be romantic. You're only my running mate."

"Stop it. You made a deal with the Prez."

"Let go of my collar . . . I'm gonna shove you off the ticket. Get rid of you. You're a walking calamity."

"Michael, listen to me. The fuckers can't hurt you. You stole from your law firm, who cares? We'll call it a loan. The Prez had a man killed. The Bull was involved. I'll nail their asses if they go near J. Michael Storm."

"You? You can't even protect a mouse."

"Don't give up on us."

"Isaac, they have all the evidence. I was a stupid fuck."

"Fight him, J. Please. The Prez will fall. Fight him."

"I can't. But you can have Marianna until the end of the month. And be careful. They got tons of crap on you too."

He kissed Isaac on the forehead. "Crazy man, you were the best rabbi I ever had."

And he vanished from the mansion, with his retainers dragging behind him, while Isaac muttered to himself, "President Storm, President Storm."

20

Calder could have met with Michael in San Diego or another Republican stronghold, but he wanted to drive the first debate into the heart of Democratic country. He chose the Grand Ballroom at the Waldorf. He could ride right down to the debate from the Presidential Suite. Fuck the polls. He was the most powerful man in the world. Michael had to give in to all of his wishes. Tim Seligman didn't say a word. There would only be one bandleader at the debate. Renata Jones, a black political journalist from the *Kansas City Star.* She would pose all the questions, time the two gladiators, cut them off if they were verbose. It was a great coup for the Prez. A black woman from middle America who couldn't be considered hostile to J. Michael Storm. Calder was going to press his urban crusade, crush Michael . . .

He slept in the White House, with Margaret Tolstoy's wigs and high heels in his closet. He wasn't a fetishist. But he loved the smell of shoe leather, Margaret's shoe leather. He invited reporters to breakfast. He had a soft-boiled egg with cameras in his face. The cameras followed him to the South Lawn, where he and Pamela Box got on the presidential helicopter, *Marine One*, and rode to Andrews Air Force Base. He chatted with his National Security Advisor and his favorite generals, who boarded *Air Force One* with him and Pam, accompanied the Prez to JFK. He wasn't reclusive. He hopped onto a bus leaving the airport, rode into Manhattan with the passengers, sang campfire songs, while the Secret Service went a little crazy trying to protect Calder Cottonwood. He kissed everyone on the bus, handed out ballpoint pens, arrived at the Waldorf around noon, and lunched at the Bull & Bear. He was in a battling mood. He didn't even bother to nap. He rehearsed the debate with his advisors, had Pam play Renata Jones, and let a tough young undersecretary be Michael Storm. The generals clapped while Calder fielded questions. Bull Latham arrived. They hovered over coffee in the sitting room. The Prez showered, changed clothes. His technical crew told Calder about the microphones in the Grand Ballroom. A team of makeup women prepared him for the cameras. He giggled, sang songs with them. The generals were amazed. They hadn't seen Calder so ebullient since his first weeks at the White House.

"A big win," they muttered. "He's gonna grab the whole goddamn cake."

The vice-president arrived, Teddy Neems, a bagman and bill collector for the Republican Party. Calder wanted to drop him, add Bull Latham to the ticket, but it might have looked as if he was scared of Sidel. And Bull was much more valuable to him at the Bureau. Bull was almost like a shadow vice-president. Bull could wear a gun in public, like Sidel. And he had the aura of the Dallas Cowboys.

Pamela coached the Prez one last time. "Mr. President, he's a skinny little prick. Look J. Michael right in the eye. You'll wither him."

She brushed lint off the President's suit. He growled at her. "Quit pawing me."

One of his undersecretaries wagged his head. "Sir, the pigeon's landed. Michael's in the hotel."

"Let him wait."

Calder smoked a cigarette. He was dreaming of Margaret Tolstoy. She'd stopped telling him stories. He couldn't seem to have an erection without Margaret. The chief urologist at Bethesda Naval Hospital had promised miracles, a painless injection that could give him a horse's prong for a whole hour. But he preferred Margaret's stories. Even the Bull couldn't catch her. Margaret was floating somewhere between Pennsylvania Avenue and Carl Schurz Park, in one of her wigs.

Pam saw the sadness in his eyes. "Mr. President, please don't drift."

"Shut up . . . I'm ready for Michael Storm."

They went down to the Grand Ballroom in three elevator cars. He kept Teddy Neems near the back of the entourage. He strode into the ballroom with his generals, Pam, and the Bull. There was a blitzkrieg of lights in his eyes. He waved his arm, and the lights disappeared. He saw Sidel. He could afford to smile.

"How are you, soldier?"

"Calder," Isaac said, "don't you think Marilyn should have stuck with Joe DiMaggio? Joltin' Joe was the love of her life."

— 187 —

The Prez grabbed Isaac's elbow. "Soldier, I agree."

Then he mounted the platform at the front of the ball-room and revealed his full height. There was a murmur in the balconies. The audience clapped.

"Ladies and gentlemen," Pam said, "the President of the United States."

He was Lincolnesque again. He stood behind the podium with the presidential seal, saluted J. Michael, and rushed over to Renata Jones, shook her hand. Cameras clicked. He returned to his podium. J. Michael was already sweating under the klieg lights. He looked like a runt. Michael's cheeks were pale. His tie was crooked. He didn't seem to know what to do with his hands.

Calder was delighted. Shithead, he muttered to himself.

Renata Jones stood to one side, tall, elegant, the Prez's handpicked black beauty. She discussed the ground rules of the debate, introduced Michael and the Prez. The runt seemed lost behind his podium.

Renata turned to face Calder Cottonwood. "Mr. President, you have two minutes to make your opening remarks."

He winked at her. "Mrs. Jones, if I babble too long, come over and spank me. The country would love to see a journalist spank the President of the United States."

The entire ballroom laughed. He'd broken that terrible static at the beginning of a presidential debate. The audience belonged to him. Michael plucked at his collar. The poor son of a bitch was all alone up there.

"Wounds," Calder said, "we have to heal the wounds. I've made mistakes. We all have. But I want to rebuild America, and I'm starting here, in the badlands of Manhattan, which Mayor Sidel's own police force has helped me reclaim."

He saw Barton Grossvogel in the audience, with a bandage under his eyes. He had to discourage Bart from joining the entourage. He couldn't go around with a mutilated man. But he'd fix Sidel. A fucking rat had bitten off Bart's nose.

"Candidate Storm," Renata said, "it's your turn now."

Michael wiped his forehead. "Thank you, ma'am, but I'll forgo an introduction . . . I might need those two minutes later on."

Fucking fool, Calder sang to himself.

"Then we'll begin," Renata said. "Mr. Storm, there's been much speculation about your past. I won't beg the question. You were the chairman of a radical organization, the Ho Chi Minh Club, while a student at Columbia University. You seized the office of the university's president, held him hostage. You damaged property, led a student revolt. Can you clarify the circumstances for us? I understand that it was a tumultuous time. But like my colleagues on the *Star*, I have to wonder if an ex-Marxist like yourself *ought* to be president."

"Ma'am," Michael said from behind his podium, "I wonder too. I did wild things. But I was never disrespectful to the soldiers and sailors and airmen of the United States. I wanted to bring them home, ma'am. I didn't want them to die in Vietnam. I lost a brother in that war, two cousins. And I heard professors utter vacuous, inhuman remarks. I watched them run to the White House and the State Department with their silly advice. More soldiers, tougher diplomacy. But they weren't willing to give up their own lives. I was. I would have stayed in that president's office until my own doom caught up with me. Was I foolish? Yes. Wrong? Perhaps. But one man walked right through the barricades, faced the anger of my fellow radicals, risked his life, left his gun with another cop. That's my running mate, Isaac Sidel, who didn't want bloodshed, didn't want to break students' heads."

The Prez looked at Renata. Damn you, cut him off.

"It was Isaac who kept me out of jail, who convinced the court that I was acting upon my own beliefs, that I wasn't trying to destroy society, but make it more democratic, more responsive to our needs."

Calder watched the TV cameras pan on Isaac Sidel, who sat in the front row with the fucking little first lady, a Glock sticking out of his pants.

"Was I immature?" Michael asked. "Then Isaac matured me. And I wouldn't be here on this platform without him."

"Thank you, Mr. Candidate," Renata said. "I think—"

"Ma'am, I'll take another minute, do my introduction now. The President talks about the badlands he'd like to rebuild. I congratulate him, and I'd ask Isaac Sidel to help him any way he can. But it's not so simple, ma'am. Good people died in those badlands, innocent people that no one has bothered to mourn."

The Prez stared at Bull Latham. Michael was on the counterattack, wasn't caving in as the Bull had promised. Then he glanced through the glare, saw Captain Knight sitting between Tim Seligman and J. Michael's whore of a wife, and all the brilliance and glamour went out of the Prez. The fuckers had set him up. He couldn't even ask the Secret Service to grab the man who'd tried to murder him. The captain would sing one song too many. Assassinations in the President's name. Illegal bloodletting. Calder's body began to tilt. He was almost stooping. The Lincolnesque profile was gone. He'd already stopped listening to Michael Storm.

21

Isaac was the babe in the woods, Sinbad, an expendable sailor. But he was still proud of J. The kid was like a wrecking crew. He'd danced around Renata Jones and stabbed Calder into a kind of dumbfounded silence.

The Prez closed his curtains, withdrew into the White House, left Teddy Neems to dangle by himself. And Isaac had to fly to Los Angeles for *his* debate at the Beverly Wilshire. Tim had commandeered the whole first-class cabin of Sinbad's plane. Isaac wouldn't sit with him, but Timmy followed Sinbad from seat to seat.

"I was your straw man."

"Isaac, we did what we had to do."

"I want Barton Grossvogel dragged out of Elizabeth Street."

"We aren't wizards. There's a limit to where we can reach. Your PC isn't in our pocket . . . not yet."

"You can't buy Sweets. He'll break your bones. I'll go into Elizabeth Street myself."

"That's brilliant. Grossvogel will eat you alive."

"What about Bull Latham? Can't the Bull sock Bart?"

"Not while Calder is in the White House."

"Then I'm beside myself," Isaac said. "I can't sleep . . . not until we've recaptured Bart's precinct."

His head dropped suddenly. He began to snore. He wasn't on the plane when he woke. He was on Sunset Boulevard in a big sedan. He sat with the little first lady and Tim, Joe Montaigne and Martin Boyle on the jump seats. People stood on both sides of the boulevard, waving to Isaac and Marianna Storm.

"Sinbad," they said, "Sinbad the Sailor."

They arrived in Westwood. "Stop the tank," Isaac said, and he went searching for Marilyn Monroe's grave. There was a simple marker built into the wall of the cemetery:

MARILYN MONROE
1926–1962

Isaac placed two pennies on the ground near Marilyn's grave. It was an old policeman's superstition: pennies to protect the dead. He returned to the sedan, shouted at Martin Boyle, "Get me the White House, will ya?"

"Isaac," Tim said, "don't give me grief. Calder hasn't recovered from the debate. He talks to no one."

"He'll talk to me."

Isaac clutched the phone, sang "Sidel here," and waited until Calder Cottonwood got onto the line.

"Mr. President, I just returned from Marilyn's grave. I left two pennies near the wall. From both of us."

"That's kind of you . . . Isaac, be gentle with Teddy Neems. He has a weak heart. I'm not sure he can survive the excitement of a televised debate."

"Calder, I can't hold his hand."

"Nurse him along. That's all I ask. Good-bye."

Isaac rode in silence to the Bev Wilshire, where Steve Mc-Queen had lived like a recluse during the last year of his life. *Bullitt* was the Big Guy's favorite film. McQueen's a cop who barely says a word, like Isaac's own lost adjutant, Manfred Coen. Coen had died in one of the police wars Isaac himself had arranged. He was still mourning Manfred Coen.

Marianna got into her bathing suit and rushed off to the pool with Joe Montaigne. Tim Seligman had booked a pair of suites in the penthouse. Isaac had a marble bathtub, with faucets made of silver and gold. He felt like some penny-ante Nero with palm trees under his window. It could have been hurricane weather. The trees bent into the wind. But the sun was out on Wilshire Boulevard. The hurricane was inside Isaac's own head. His conversation with Calder had been a subterfuge. Both of them were desperate without Margaret Tolstoy.

He went down to the bar, had to duck Martin Boyle and Tim Seligman for a few moments. He was thinking of Margaret and the dark chocolate she adored. Uncle Ferdinand had to risk his own life and rob from the Gestapo to find black chocolate for his little bride in Odessa, bricks of chocolate that were much more valuable than human blood. "Son," Isaac asked the barman, who was about sixty years old, "do you have black chocolate?"

The barman didn't even blink. "I can find you some, Mr. Sidel. This is the Bev."

The barman returned with a tiny brick of chocolate on a gold-rimmed plate, a napkin, a knife, a fork, and a glass of low-fat milk. A woman came up to Sinbad, sat on the next stool. Isaac was trembling. She looked like Margaret.

"Sidel," she said, "I can't stay very long."

It was Pamela Box, wearing one of Margaret's wigs.

"Will you share some of my chocolate?"

"I hate the stuff. I can't afford to have Tim find me. He'll make a fuss."

"Don't worry. I talked to the Prez. I won't hurt Teddy Neems."

"It's not Neems I'm worried about. It's you."

"Ah, I've inherited a fairy godmother."

"Not quite . . . keep on your toes. You have kamikazes behind you. That's why Margaret disappeared. I had to send her on a mission. She's been killing all the kamikazes she can. There are only a couple left."

"Who hired these kamikazes?"

"That's the problem. I'm not sure. The Prez was at a meeting with his people. The Bull was there. And Bart Grossvogel. Calder was having one of his fits. He talked of *settling* Isaac Sidel. It was as simple as that. The machinery got into motion. There was a special team, attached to some agency that isn't even in the phone book. The point is that the team can't be recalled once it's set in motion. Not even Bull can stop the chaos, and he's tried."

"Is Marianna in danger? Because if she is, I'll . . ."

"No," Pam said. "The kamikazes are quite strict. One target, and only one."

"And Calder knows?"

"Dammit. He's forgotten all about your death sentence. And if I remind him, he'll go over the edge. And we'll have a schizoid in the White House."

"So I have to watch out for the fucking wind . . . can't even eat my chocolate. It could be spiked."

"The kamikazes kill with their hands. That's the one solid bit of info we have."

She touched Isaac's hair. "I can understand why Margaret loves you." And she was gone, like the wind off a palm tree. Isaac wanted to go out to the pool, watch Marianna swim, but he was like a poisoned object who might sting anyone around him, thanks to the kamikazes.

He returned to his suite. People began to flit around him. Any one of them could have been a candidate to strangle Isaac. But how could he recognize the hands of a kamikaze?

"Fuck it," he said. He put on a silk suit. He lent himself to the makeup girl. He didn't need advisors. He could demolish Teddy in his dreams. Marianna accompanied him to the Bev's ballroom. She was wearing a tiara and a white dress.

"Darling, this is my last engagement. Bring me Alyosha, or get yourself another girl."

Isaac's head was fuzzy. He put his arm around Marianna, shielded her from whatever kamikazes might be around. It wasn't much of a debate. The cameras never left Isaac. He had to hug Teddy Neems, or the vice-president might have disappeared into his own private hurricane.

"I'm a cop," Isaac said. "I know how to fight. Sometimes it gets dirty. I wish I knew some other way . . ."

There was a party at the pool. Isaac stared at the woman who fed him hors d'oeuvres. She had one brown eye and one blue. He noticed the horseshoe triceps under her uniform. "What's your name?" he asked.

"Kate."

She was the kamikaze. Isaac was almost serene, imagining the battle that would take place. He welcomed it. He kissed Marianna good night, whistled on his ride upstairs to the penthouse. He got into bed with his gun. There was a knock on the door.

He opened up, stood in his pajamas, stared into a brown eye. "Come in, Kate."

He didn't even wonder when he saw her white gloves. But he expected a tiny bit of foreplay, and he got none. She banged into Isaac, and the Glock fell out of his waistband. She kicked him in the groin and thrust a wire around his neck. But Isaac managed to catch two fingers under the wire, or she would have torn his neck off. He danced around the room, noticed the Microbe's alligator belt on the back of a Louis Quatorze chair. He clutched the belt with his left hand, swung it like a battle chain, and clipped Kate on her blue eye with the buckle.

Isaac had to forget that she was a woman. He walloped her again. The blue eye closed. He wrapped the belt around her throat, pulled at both ends with all his might, and strangled the strangler.

He deposited her in the closet, called Martin Boyle and Joe

Montaigne, showed them the body. "Lads, you'll have to get rid of her."

"No problem," said Joe Montaigne. "Sir, is she a kamikaze? There were rumors. We didn't know what to believe."

"Grand," Isaac said. "I have two bodyguards who let me freelance on my own."

They wheeled Kate out the door in a laundry cart.

Isaac had a nasty cut on his neck. The night porter arrived with balls of cotton and a bottle of hydrogen peroxide. Isaac was cautious. He couldn't face another kamikaze.

The telephone rang at two A.M. Tim Seligman must have heard about the little *accident* in Isaac's suite. But it wasn't Timmy. Marianna was calling.

"Darling," she said, "I can't stop thinking of Alyosha."

22

Suicide girls. Sidel didn't care how many kamikazes he met. He'd rip them off the streets of Beverly Hills, dance with them on Rodeo Drive. The Big Guy was worried about Margaret Tolstoy. He was no Cassandra. He stopped dreaming of rats and red harpoons. But he'd always been a baseball addict. Isaac knew his stats. Not even a demigod like DiMaggio could sock home runs forever. The immortals had to strike out.

He shivered when Martin Boyle knocked on his door at the Bev. Isaac was taking a bath. He climbed out of the tub, unlocked the door, and couldn't blind himself to the dread marks on Boyle's face.

"Margaret's down, isn't she, Boyle?"

"She was rushed to Bellevue, Mr. President."

"Is she alive?"

The Secret Service man shrugged his shoulders.

Isaac had to ask again. "Is she alive?"

"Barely, sir. She's in a coma. She took a terrible crack on the head."

"I thought the kamikazes only strangle people."

"Correct. They strangle their victims, but not their pursuers, sir."

Isaac was scheduled to toss the opening ball at Dodger Stadium, but he got on the earliest flight out of L.A. with Marianna and their two babysitters, while Tim was snoring at the Bev. Isaac wouldn't eat on the plane, wouldn't even give his autograph to a little girl. He was at Bellevue's critical ward in under six hours. Margaret lay with an enormous bandage wrapped around her head, like a beautiful mummy. A little blood leaked out of the bandage. She was connected to a couple of machines. Her almond eyes recognized nothing. Isaac was only one more person in the room.

Bull Latham was at her bedside.

"What happened?" Isaac growled.

"We don't know. We found her in the badlands, mumbling on Sheriff Street."

"Mumbling on Sheriff Street. Near Barton Grossvogel's barn."

"Isaac, it wasn't Bart. His own men called in the attack."

"After they pistol-whipped her, dented Margaret's skull."

"And could have totaled her, but they didn't. Your logic sucks. Bart's men saved her life . . . I had to tell the Prez. He was crying when he heard about Margaret."

"Wonderful. He gave the order to have me bumped. And you listened, Bull. You sent out the kamikazes."

"Kamikazes. That's a myth."

"Was it a myth that tried to strangle me at the Bev

Wilshire? Margaret was crushing them, one by one. Who's their leader, who trains them?"

"There are no kamikazes. And even if there were, that's classified."

Isaac rushed at the Bull, and three nurses had to hold him.

"You'll have to leave, Mr. Mayor. We can't take care of Mrs. Tolstoy while you're around."

Isaac left the hospital. He had nowhere to go. He went to Elizabeth Street. The desk sergeant smiled when he saw Isaac, didn't even ask him to remove his Glock.

"You can go upstairs, Mr. Sidel. The captain's expecting you."

Detectives saluted him, got out of his way. Their sudden politeness disturbed Isaac. It felt like the overture to a kill. He walked into Barton's office. The captain's bandages moved on his face like a little white whale. "Glad you could make it."

"I've been meaning to visit," Isaac said. "Regards from Raskolnikov."

"You've got a pair of balls on you, mentioning that rat."

A bunch of cops arrived from another door. They didn't menace Isaac, simply surrounded him. But he still had a touch of vertigo.

"You're running kamikazes from this stationhouse," Isaac said. "This is the storage battery."

"Think so, Mr. Mayor? If I'm that important, why the fuck are you still alive? I lost half my nose because of you. I'll wear these wounds into the grave."

"Cap," one of Barton's soldiers said, "can't we do the little politician?"

"Not today."

That wasn't Bart. It was a voice that shot into Isaac's back. Isaac couldn't maneuver among all those cops, but he could recognize the melody of Bernardo Dublin. Bernardo dug a path to Isaac with his elbows.

"Ah," Bart said, "your rescuer's arrived. From the Democratic camp . . . how's Clarice?"

"Shove it, Bart," Bernardo said and marched Isaac out of Elizabeth Street.

"Margaret's in a coma," Isaac said. "The bastards almost beat her to death."

"And you're gonna battle a whole police station?"

"Wouldn't you?"

Bernardo laughed. "Yeah. That's because I was trained by a superidealist, Isaac Sidel."

"I'll need guards in front of Margaret's bed. Night and day."

"Boss, Sweets has already handled it. Nobody can get near her."

"Then why was Bull Latham right in her room?"

"Boss, he's FBI."

"But he could have trained whoever got to Margaret."

"Possibly," Bernardo said. "But he's not stupid. He has to back off."

"Bernardo, I want you on the case. It was no ordinary geek that she met in the badlands. A geek couldn't have gotten that close to Margaret, a geek couldn't have knocked her in the head. That fucking brief encounter had to be with someone she already knew."

"Boss, I'll look. I'll ask. But I can't waltz around Clarice. She pages me every half hour."

Who else could Isaac have trusted but a killer cop like Bernardo Dublin? He could only draw a company of badasses around him. "Bernardo," he said, "just do what you can, okay?"

Isaac hugged Bernardo and returned to Bellevue, visited the chief pathologist. He wanted to examine the X rays of Margaret's skull. The pathologist shouted at his assistants, who scurried around, then whispered in the pathologist's ear.

The pathologist glanced at the wall. "Isaac, the X rays are missing."

"Stolen, you mean. They've been lifted from Bellevue."

"Nothing like that. It's sloppiness. They'll turn up. They've been misplaced."

Isaac grabbed the pathologist's neck. "A woman is lying in a coma, and you can't even come up with her X rays. Take me to the doc who admitted Margaret."

"Isaac, what can he tell you? He's a nobody, a boy."

"Take me to him, and get the fuck out of my sight."

Isaac sat in a tiny room with a young black intern, Rufus Rowe, who wore wire glasses and had delicate hands.

"Doc, was she hit with a blunt instrument, like a hammer?"

"No. The lacerations didn't suggest that. There was another pattern. I'm not a pathologist, but I'd say that she was struck once behind the ear and then kicked."

"She was stamped on," Isaac said, "stomped."

"Yes, savagely kicked, not once or twice, but many, many times."

Isaac's dizziness had come back. He thanked the intern, but the Big Guy could barely walk. He had a habit of manufacturing his own angels of death.

"Ah," he said, "my beloved Bernardo."

It was the signature of the Bronx brigade. That's how Bernardo Dublin destroyed half his own gang. He'd stomped them to death. And then Alyosha would paint their pictures on a wall.

How did Bernardo get to Elizabeth Street so fast, pull him away from Bart? It was all rehearsed. Bernardo had a much more subtle rabbi than Isaac Sidel. He belonged to Bull Latham.

Isaac rushed upstairs to Margaret, held her hand. And Sinbad the Sailor started to cry.

He was back in public school, with Margaret Tolstoy, who called herself Anastasia and bewitched the entire class. What could mansions mean to him, the brouhaha of worldly power, next to Anastasia's smile? She appeared one day out of the blue, with holes in her socks, and the bearing of a princess. She'd studied ballet. She'd lived in Paris, starved in Odessa, and Isaac hadn't even crossed the Williamsburg Bridge.

When she vanished without a word, he fell into a state of shock. Isaac couldn't recover, no matter how many cases he solved, how many people he glocked . . . until Anastasia reappeared, like a divine accident that had probably been arranged by the FBI.

She opened her almond eyes. He was still clutching her hand. He'd been with her two days, had barely washed, grabbed sandwiches from a nurse. Her hand moved in Isaac's. She tried to speak.

"Shhh," he said. "It's all right. I know it was Bernardo Dublin."

There was almost a smile under that mummy's mask of hers. She whispered a couple of words. Isaac couldn't read her lips. She gripped his hand a little tighter.

"Darling," she said. "Danger."

And she drifted back into sleep. Her almond eyes must have returned to Odessa, where that stinking bureaucrat, Antonescu, had built a ballet school in a world without carrots or potatoes or borscht. Anastasia danced in a desert . . .

Isaac sat in the dark, waited. Ah, he heard a noise. It had to be Bernardo, skulking back to finish the job before Margaret had the chance to come out of her coma. Bernardo could get through the police detail outside Margaret's door. All he had to do was show his shield.

But it wasn't Bernardo. Another badass wandered through the door.

"How are you, homey?" Isaac asked from his privileged seat in the dark.

"Uncle Isaac," Alyosha said. He didn't seem startled.

"Who let you out of Peekskill Manor?"

"I escaped."

"Homey, you shouldn't lie . . . you're Bernardo's little man, aren't you? It was Bernardo who let you out of that reform school. And he couldn't have done it with a gold shield from the NYPD. They don't like New York City cops in Peekskill. He had another fucking ID."

"I think so," Alyosha said. "A piece of plastic."

"With the FBI's insignia and coat of arms."

"Uncle," Alyosha said, "everybody's scared of the FBI."

"And what was your mission, homey?"

"To see if the bald lady was still alive."

"She isn't bald," Isaac said. "She has to cut her hair short . . . but how did you get past the detail of cops?"

"They know me, Uncle. They've seen me with you."

"And Bernardo counted on that, didn't he? That the cops would consider you my own little man. How much is he paying you?"

"Don't talk silver, Uncle. Bernardo rescued me from that children's jail in the Bronx."

"And destroyed your brother's gang."

"Can't be helped. That's the casualties of war."

"Homey, I took you into the Merliners, I let you live in my mansion."

"I know," Alyosha said. "But I met him before I met you . . . in the Bronx."

"And a Bronx cavalier had to figure what Bernardo would do if the lady opened her eyes."

"Yeah, I figured."

"And it didn't even matter how that kind of shit might have hurt me."

"It mattered," Alyosha said. "I wasn't gonna tell Bernardo much. But I had to come here. He would have broken my neck."

"Where is he? Where's the prince?"

"On Sutton Place. With Clarice."

"And you were gonna phone him the news, huh? Bernardo's messenger boy . . . you disappointed me, homey."

Isaac handed Alyosha to one of the guards outside the door. "Chain him to your chair. I'll be right back."

Isaac dialed his chauffeur. "Mullins, get your ass down to Bellevue. You're gonna ride Angel Carpenteros back to Peekskill Manor. And I don't want you to do it alone. Bring two or three cops from the mansion."

"Boss, is the kid public enemy number one?"

"That's exactly what you're gonna tell the folks at Peekskill. He gets no privileges. He stays in his room. And if somebody shows up with plastic from the FBI, I want to hear about it."

Isaac returned to Margaret Tolstoy, kissed her eyes, and ran out of Bellevue.

He didn't get much flak from Clarice. She'd had a love affair all afternoon with the vodka in her fridge. He squeezed a couple of limes for her, and when she started to wobble, he carried her to the couch. "Where's Bernardo?" she asked. "Where's my sex slave?"

"I'll find him."

"You'll have to salute me, you son of a bitch. I'll make your life miserable soon as I'm First Lady. You'll sleep in a tent."

"I'm like a Bedouin. I adore tents."

Isaac didn't have to prowl across the apartment. It was Bernardo who found him.

"I had a little talk with your homey," Isaac said.

There wasn't even a ripple in Bernardo's red mustache. He walked Isaac out onto the terrace to avoid the different bugs in Clarice's walls.

"How's my favorite fucking kamikaze?"

"I'm no strangler, boss."

"How did the Bull get to you, turn you around?"

"Simple. He caught me selling drugs."

"Was it after Michael hired you to kill Clarice?"

"Before," Bernardo said, "long before."

"Jesus Christ. Then it was Bull Latham who had you destroy your old gang."

"Sure," Bernardo said. "It was part of the President's plan."

"Bull ran the Bronx brigade?"

"Boss, I don't know how many feds were involved. Don't feel bad. They fuck everybody."

"Bull was monitoring your adventures with Clarice. He was right in the heart of Democratic country. So why the hell are we going to win?"

"Calder's unstable. He showed his prick to a couple of grandmas. He walked around naked in the middle of a White House tour. The Secret Service had to hide him in a toilet. Bull decided to deal with the Dems."

"And get rid of Isaac Sidel."

"It's complicated, boss. The Prez was needling him. Called Bull a pussy. Said he couldn't wind your clock. Bull made one phone call, and kamikazes start coming out of the woodwork."

"Who the fuck are they?"

"Ex-Marines. A lady wrestler. Nasty mothers who travel from agency to agency . . ."

"And you've been monitoring them. You're their fucking liaison with the Bureau. You probably have a code name."

"Santa Claus."

"That's grand," Isaac said. "Did you train with them?"

"Once or twice."

"Cut it out," Isaac said. "You're their paymaster. Bull unleashes them to pacify the Prez."

"That's about it."

"Then finish the job," Isaac said, standing against the terrace wall. "Kill me."

"I can't," Bernardo said. "I wouldn't know how."

"You knew how to stomp on Margaret. Why isn't she dead?"

"I didn't have my heart in it."

"But you plucked Alyosha out of Peekskill and sent him to look at Margaret."

"Boss, if she wakes up, she could remember me, and I'd have complications."

"She already woke up. And she didn't have to remember. I recognized your rotten trademark. Bernardo Dublin, the man who steps on people . . ."

Isaac wanted to rip him off at the ears, hurl Bernardo over the edge of the balcony, send him into another kingdom, but he couldn't. Bernardo was one of his own, a homicidal child. And Isaac was a politician now. Clarice would crack without Bernardo. America would have a mad First Lady.

"Boss, she was closing in on the kamikazes. She would have connected me to them, thought I was a kamikaze who lived in Bull's closet."

The Big Guy clutched one of Bernardo's ears. "Who am I, homey?"

"Sinbad."

"And what can Sinbad expect from his little sailor?"

"Every fucking word the Bull whispers in my ear."

Isaac left him on the balcony with Clarice's jungle plants and traveled as far as he could from Sutton Place South.

23

He had his own private room in the country club for bad boys, Peekskill Manor. The Big Guy wouldn't let the courts return him to that Bronx shelter where he had to wear lipstick for the guards. No one touched Alyosha. He could order milk shakes, eat bowls of ice cream, but he couldn't leave his room. Most of the other bad boys were rich, came from families who arrived in chauffeured limousines. They'd never heard of the Bronx, didn't even know what a barrio was, and Alyosha had to live around strangers who hadn't seen his wall art, his memorials to dead Latin Jokers, Jokers he had helped to kill.

Marianna would move into the White House in a couple of months, and Alyosha was a boy without a country. The Big Guy hated him for becoming Bernardo's rat, would never bring Marianna around again. Alyosha would have died without his crayons and pieces of colored chalk. He'd mark up the walls, like Michelangelo. But he didn't have a ladder in Peekskill, or any church to play with. He had nothing but his room in the bad boys' hotel.

He was much too sad to sketch his lost country of the Bronx, and so he used the walls around him to recreate the badlands where that savior in the orange pants had been killed. He drew the stones, the dead streets, housing projects like thick, heavy needles scratching the sky. He drew the police station that stood at the edge of the badlands like some murderous lighthouse. He thrust the Brooklyn Bridge and the canyons of Wall Street into the background. But he wouldn't draw people, not the young pyromaniacs who torched whatever isolated garden they could find, not the drug addicts, not the crazy, screaming old women and men, not the cops, not Benya Krik. It was only Alyosha himself who inhabited the gardenless garden on his walls, like some warden of the underworld. It couldn't make him happy, but all his furious markings kept his mind off Marianna.

And while he colored in the last remaining patches, he heard a voice.

"The Maldavanka. I can't believe it."

It was the Big Guy, groaning as usual. Marianna was with him, and Alyosha hadn't even noticed, that's how blind his art could make him.

"Don't I get a kiss?"

The crayon broke in his hand. He wanted to cry. He hugged Marianna, whirled her around his fancy cell.

"Darling," she said, while she was still in Alyosha's arms, "can't you disappear? I have things to discuss with my fiancé."

"Marianna, you know the rules. If I leave, you have to leave with me."

"Then shut your eyes, or crawl under the bed."

Alyosha smiled. Isaac was almost as human as Raskolnikov, the rat who lived in a shoebox. "Marianna, don't be hard on the Big Guy. He's practically given his life to the United States."

"And what about me? I have to walk with him, hand in hand. My feet hurt, and I never get to see you . . . Uncle Isaac, can't you get him out of this hellhole?"

"No court will give him to me. And if we steal Alyosha, we'll lose all control and he'll end up in a joint with barbed wire. Peekskill Manor isn't such a hellhole."

"It is to me," Marianna said.

He couldn't walk away with Alyosha, and he didn't want to. That Bronx cavalier was still devoted to Bernardo, but Marianna was in love with him. And Isaac couldn't even close his eyes. A kamikaze might come into the room. He had to stroll around like some sheriff with his finger near his gun. Margaret couldn't kill kamikazes while she was in a coma, and she couldn't return to Isaac's bed. He'd have to kidnap her from the hospital one of these days, ask her to become his personal huntress. They'd hunt in the Maldavanka, in the frozen fields. To hell with the White House. Isaac and his lady would hunt for love. Ah, what's the use? The fucking Democrats would find them . . .

Alyosha stared at Isaac. "Uncle, don't be sad. The whole rotten planet's a prison cell."

The leaves had started to fall. Isaac could already feel winter in his bones. The election was two weeks away. People couldn't stop clutching his hand. He was hooked into the Democratic circuit again. Michael called him every afternoon.

"Kid, they're talking landslide. Calder won't even take Texas . . . or his home state."

"Michael, let's not gloat. Calder might surprise us."

"He's a dead man."

And Isaac began to believe in J. Barton Grossvogel lost his footing on Elizabeth Street. He was shoved out of the precinct, offered a captaincy in the Bronx. He grabbed his pension, retired. The Bull had deserted Calder and signaled to the NYPD that he wanted Bart out of the way. Isaac danced in his own bedroom . . . until he discovered the name of the new captain. Douglas Knight had come out of retirement to pilot Elizabeth Street. And Isaac felt betrayed.

The Dems had been dealing behind his back. He didn't even go downtown to congratulate Captain Knight. He avoided Elizabeth Street. Barton's gang was still there. Sweets should have flopped the whole precinct, but he couldn't tamper with Calder Cottonwood's favorite toy.

Isaac abandoned his schedule. He wouldn't fly to Albuquerque with the little first lady and address a bunch of environmentalists. He went into the Maldavanka. He could only breathe in the badlands. He couldn't find one falling leaf. He had the memory of Alyosha's mural in his head. Alyosha had drawn a black moon over the Maldavanka. Isaac felt like a citizen of that moon . . . with a rat he carried in a shoebox under his arm. Soon he'd have his own staff at the White House, his own suite that Martin Boyle had already nicknamed The Kremlin.

"Sir," Boyle had said, "Michael won't be able to maneuver around you."

"Boyle, he'll bury me."

"Not Sinbad the Sailor. Not Sidel."

Isaac kept walking under Alyosha's black moon. A police car bumped behind him. Captain Knight climbed out of the car, wearing medals that Bart Grossvogel might have worn.

"Cap, keep away from me."

"You didn't even come to my housewarming. Sweets was there."

"What about Tim Seligman? He's your godfather. It was Tim who choreographed that stunt at the Waldorf, wasn't it?"

"No. I'd come to kill the President. But Isaac Sidel got in the way. You saw my escape route. I used the kitchen."

"And I found ten or fifteen chefs. You were one of them. It was Timmy who'd arranged that little cooking school."

"You're blind. It wasn't Tim. I hid in a closet. Isaac, that kitchen was a mile long."

"Nobody arrests you. Sweets tears up your retirement papers. And you're back in harness, right where Dougy worked."

"Did I have a choice? How long would I have survived without the Democrats?"

"It was a lalapalooza, sitting next to Timmy at the first debate, in the same fucking hotel where you'd nearly whacked the Prez."

"That was Michael's touch."

"I can imagine. He almost brought down Columbia University . . . Doug, what the hell are you doing here?"

"I can finish what Dougy started."

"He was an outcast in orange pants. You're a police captain with all of Barton Grossvogel's gang."

"I'll scatter them, Isaac, one or two at a time . . . I'll help the poor, bring life back into the badlands. Trust me."

The captain returned to Elizabeth Street. And for an instant Isaac wished he had his own Odessa and could become a bandit who burnt down police stations. But he was only a guy with a Glock. Isaac Sidel. A shadow seemed to flirt with him, shove in and out of the Maldavanka's dunes. "Of course," Isaac muttered. Where else would a kamikaze trap him? Who would have heard Isaac's screams at his own little strangulation party? Was it a man this time? Or another woman with horseshoe triceps?

"What's your name?"

"Martin Boyle."

"Jesus," Isaac said, "are you following me? I thought you were a strangler."

"I'm paid to follow you, sir."

Isaac let Raskolnikov out of the shoebox. The rat jumped into the air and landed on Isaac's neck. His eyes seemed to burn in the blue dusk.

"You won't be able to bring him into the White House, sir."

"I'm aware of that. But I'd like to enjoy Raskolnikov while I can."

And Isaac plunged deeper into the dusk, like some hooky player who would soon be sentenced to four full years of school. He didn't hear the familiar shuffle of a Secret Service man's shoes.

"Are you still with me, Boyle?"

He couldn't hear a sound.

"Are you with me?"

"Yes, Mr. President."